The Tall Tales of
Dracula's Daggers

Dracula's Revenge

Other titles by Gary Morecambe:

The Tall Tales of
Dracula's Daggers

Dracula's Revenge

Gary Morecambe

SCHOLASTIC

Scholastic Children's Books,
Commonwealth House, 1–19 New Oxford Street,
London, WC1A 1NU, UK
A division of Scholastic Ltd
London ~ New York ~ Toronto ~ Sydney ~ Auckland
Mexico City ~ New Delhi ~ Hong Kong

First published in the UK by Scholastic Ltd, 2003

ISBN 0 439 98180 8

Printed and bound in Great Britain by Cox & Wyman Ltd, Reading, Berkshire

10 9 8 7 6 5 4 3 2 1

Deadication

To Count Henry, George, Bartolemé of Buckhorn,
Westonia and London

Contents

...And the one called the Prince of Darkness
came to me on hearing of my strange powers.
The task he set before me, and over which I
had no say or control, was to create a number
of magical daggers. Daggers that would contain
inside them energy of colossal quantity, which
would then join together in one mighty force
and enter the soul of the Prince of Darkness,
making him ruler supreme of our whole planet...

Tall and proud himself, he looked a small and bent figure
in the presence of Vlad Dracula.

Chapter One

The Second Dagger

When Dracula scraped back the lid of his coffin, the light of a flickering candle danced on his sickly, transparent features. He had heard the footfalls on the cold cellar steps almost before they had happened.

"Who is it who disturbs my rest?" he asked, his voice deep and toneless.

"It is only I, oh great one," answered Count Krinkelfiend, stumbling down the stone steps.

"Why are you here?" said Dracula, a note of irritation appearing in his voice.

"Well, oh master, you summoned me here!"

Dracula slowly and carefully removed the lid completely, and emerged tall and immaculate from his coffin. "Yes, I did," he said, looking Krinkelfiend in the eye.

"I was so excited to hear from you, my master, I rushed over at once. Oh, the honour you do me is surely—"

"Be quiet, Krinkelfiend," interrupted Dracula.

"Oh, right. Sorry."

Krinkelfiend stood still. Tall and proud himself, he looked a small and bent figure in the presence of Vlad Dracula.

"I have work for you, Krinkelfiend," Dracula finally said. Krinkelfiend found it hard not to jump for joy. For the last couple of years, he had lived in the hope that he would hear such words from Vlad Dracula.

"You do, master?" he smiled. Then Krinkelfiend remembered the last time they had met. "I'm sorry about the two-headed dragon," he said.

"It was nothing," said Dracula.

"My son, Rupert, was irritating me, you see. I thought it best to frighten him a bit."

"As I have said: it was nothing."

"Yes, indeed," nodded the count. "He has never been a full vampire, you see. His mother was mortal, and—"

"As I have said – twice, already – it was nothing!"

Silence.

Dracula took a step closer to Krinkelfiend. "You recall the dagger, no doubt? You, who found it? You, who thought you had awoken me from my slumber within the dagger?"

Krinkelfiend couldn't tell if Dracula was congratulating him on the past deed, or reprimanding him. He decided to play it safe.

"Well, yes, master," he said. "Though your return from it was an accident, I have to say. I had merely read of the dagger's existence and traced it to Viktoria Palace in Gertcha, and—"

"There is a *second* dagger!" Dracula interrupted.

"A . . . *second* dagger?" gasped Krinkelfiend.

"That is why I have been inactive this last few years. I have been awaiting news from various agents I have dispersed to likely places. And now. . ." Dracula rubbed his hands together, a little how Krinkelfiend often would. "I have agents operating around the globe, and one has reported back to me from London. He has word that the dagger described has been seen on display in this city."

"This dagger, your greatness," said Krinkelfiend in a hoarse whisper. "Is it . . . powerful, too?"

"As powerful as the first," said Dracula, his dark eyes glazing over as he pictured the two identical daggers together for the first time in centuries. "Marvin the blind monk created them. Of course, it is currently inactive. It needs to be in my possession for its powers to be realized."

"But then—" began Krinkelfiend, visualizing the power Dracula would possess.

"Yes, Krinkelfiend. Then I would be the ruler of earth – nothing could prevent it. And one hundred years of darkness would reign, as the wise and remarkable Marvin predicted."

"But, my lord," said Krinkelfiend after a short pause for thought, "why did you not combine the daggers powers back in the early days – when Marvin first created them?"

Dracula tried to smile in an ironical way, but it hurt him to do so. "I turned my back on them," he admitted. "I had to. Firstly, Marvin died of some mortal illness that these human weaklings are always seeming to get. Then word reached me that my lands were under threat from my enemies. Battles were raging all over the homeland during this time."

"Where did the daggers go?" Krinkelfiend pressed gently, knowing this could be the only time he would ever find Dracula in a reflective, trance-like mood, and thus content to answer the count's questions.

"The first, as you know, I had hidden in Viktoria Palace. I knew the king. He, of course, had no idea I was a vampire. I gave him the dagger as a gift, and encouraged him to display it with his other daggers and artefacts, fully intending to one day return and claim it back when the wars were at an end. *You* saved me that task," Dracula reminded him. "The second. . ." His eyes glowed in the dim light. ". . .The second was stolen. I sensed its presence for some time after, but then that feeling faded. I realized it was lost. Lost and far from the homeland."

"I see," whispered Krinkelfiend.

"Until now!" said Dracula, suddenly spinning round to face Krinkelfiend full on.

He flicked his fingers and a dozen flame torches on the wall burst into light. "London, England, Krinkelfiend. That is where you are destined."

"Oh, thank you, my lord," bowed the count. "A busy city, I am told. Is the dagger . . . visible, shall we say?"

"Very visible. I have an agent who believes it to be on display at the British Museum."

"Oh, this is fine news indeed, master."

"My agent will fill you in on your arrival there," Dracula told him. "His name is Grog. He is unmistakeable, as you will discover."

"Very good, great one."

"But you must employ others," said Dracula. "I do not wish to hear of any slip-ups. No more interfering sons and their comrades in arms."

"What of Helsing?" said Krinkelfiend, the word uncomfortable on his tongue.

Dracula frowned. "Helsing *will* interfere for certain. It is the way of the Immortal Ones. But we can outwit him. And then, when the moment is right – when I, Vlad Dracul have command over the planet – I will be able to finally destroy him."

"Of course, master," replied Krinkelfiend. Then he began thinking of Vermyn and the two oafs that Vermyn had employed. He knew no others from the daylight world he could trust. Unfortunately, it *had* to be them.

"I know of some humans," he told Dracula. "I think they could be made available."

"Excellent. Your coffin, with *you* inside it, sails tomorrow morning." He pushed a packet into Krinkelfiend's hands. "Travel details and all the money you could possibly require."

"Thank you," said Krinkelfiend, accepting the packet.

"Good luck," said Dracula. "Grog will make contact with you in London. He will observe the harbour front at Portsmouth, where your ship will land, to be sure you are not followed."

"Yes, great one."

"And one last thing," said Dracula. "If you are thinking of returning without the dagger, then it would be best not to return at all."

Krinkelfiend gulped. What was he getting himself into in working for his lord and master?

Ten minutes later, Picklewhite found himself alone in his office with a sealed and occupied coffin.

Chapter Two

Friends and Enemies

London 1902

Percy Picklewhite, a London stockbroker's clerk, was busy sorting through a pile of paperwork when he was distracted by a knock on his office door.

"Good morning, sir," said one of two men standing in his entranceway. "Special delivery, sir. Will you sign for it?"

Picklewhite looked confused. "I wasn't expecting a special delivery," he said. "What is it? Do you know?"

"A box, sir!" replied the same man.

"A *coffin*, to be precise," said the other man.

"A – a *coffin*!" gasped Picklewhite. "Gentlemen, I really think you must have come to the wrong—"

"The deceased was boxed abroad and dispatched to your address here in London, sir," said the first man, eager to get on with the job.

"You mean to tell me that there's someone *in* the coffin?" cried Picklewhite.

"No point in burying an empty one, sir," said the first man.

Ten minutes later, Picklewhite found himself alone in his office with a sealed and occupied coffin. He crept around it, half expecting it to leap at him like a mad dog. "A coffin!" he sighed at length. "What on earth am I to do with a coffin?" For a second, he thought about removing the lid, which wasn't bolted down properly. But the thought of what poor creature might be inside made him shudder.

That evening, Picklewhite went home in a state of confusion. Who should he tell? What should he do?

During the dead of night, the occupant of the coffin emerged from his long journey across the seas. Count Krinkelfiend pushed off the lid, stood up and stretched his long thin legs and arms. "London at last," he whispered. "Clever plan to be boxed and delivered to a random address," he chuckled. "And now to find the secret address my master gave me, and get away from here."

Krinkelfiend searched Picklewhite's desk until he found the delivery receipt, which he shoved deep into his trouser pocket. Then he clicked his fingers and the coffin disappeared. Krinkelfiend turned into a bat and flew out of an open window.

Vermyn, a lifelong criminal, sat down opposite his two confederates, the Ripaka Brothers, better known as Itch and Scratch.

After Krinkelfiend had freed Vermyn from prison with a touch of vampire magic, he had suggested that Vermyn should track down his original agents. "At least they have an understanding of what I am," the count had told the grinning villain.

"Yes, your countship," Vermyn had grovelled. "A splendid idea." But he hadn't been thinking it a splendid idea at all. Those two idiot brothers nearly drove him mad when he'd employed them for the Viktoria Palace job.

"So, let's get this straight," Itch sniffed. "You're going to be our paymaster again, and this time we've got to do a bit of lookout work in London?"

"That sounds about right!" grinned Vermyn – and how he could grin. Not that he had had much to grin about while in prison. But from the moment Krinkelfiend had come in the dead of night and released him from his nightmare, he hadn't stopped grinning for more than a second or two.

"All expenses paid?" Scratch checked.

"Of course," Vermyn nodded. "Your travel documents have been prepared. You will meet me again in London at a provided address, where we will discuss details more closely."

Scratch looked at Itch, who looked back at Scratch. "Sounds all right to me, big brother," said Itch.

"Good money," agreed Scratch. "I suppose we're in, then."

Vermyn clasped his hands gently together. "Excellent, gentlemen," he said.

Professor von Morcumstein, Inspector Klaw, Helsing, Rupert and Orlov entered the compartment of their carriage. The train was going from Portsmouth Harbour – where they had recently arrived by ship – to London, Waterloo.

It was Helsing who had summoned his colleagues together for the journey to England, for it was Helsing who had been watching Dracula closely these past years. When the lord of all vampires sent an agent by ship to England, Helsing knew it would be connected to dark work going on there. And, as an Immortal One, it was Helsing's responsibility to prevent all vampires pursuing their work of darkness.

But Helsing hadn't lived four hundred years without developing agents of his own. He received a telegram saying that the man described as Dracula's agent, last seen in Transylvania, had now landed by ship in Portsmouth and had purchased a rail ticket to London. . .

"You look unhappy, Orlov," commented Helsing, as he hoisted each of their cases on to the overhead racks.

"Unhappy?" squawked Orlov. "Of *course* I'm unhappy. It's all right for you. When we last saw you outside Dracula's Castle in Bran a couple of years ago, you staggered about the place like someone who was a hundred years old. *Now* look at you! Prancing around like a thirty year old."

"That is what being an Immortal One is all about," Helsing reminded him. "I shed that mortal coil and regenerated into a young man again. This happens to me approximately every eighty or so years."

"It's not fair, that's all," moaned Orlov. "I was beautiful for about five minutes. *Now* look at me." They all looked at him, and had to agree – if only to themselves – he looked truly hideous. Ten fingers and toes on each hand and foot; a slanted nose; a hump; boils everywhere.

"We'll make you beautiful again, I promise it," Rupert reassured him.

"I hope so," grumbled Orlov. "It's the only reason I agreed to come all this way. And you said that last time, about me being beautiful. You said the dagger would do the trick."

"In a way, it did," the professor intercepted wisely. "It was just that the single dagger did not contain enough power to sustain your good looks. Certainly not as much as we had originally suspected."

"You told me it had enough power to make me beautiful."

"Well, yes," sighed Rupert. "But. . . But your beauty wore off, Orlov. That is why we are in search of the second of Dracula's daggers."

"We're in search of the second because you want to stop Dracula getting his hands on it and making himself ruler of the planet," grumbled Orlov.

"Well, that's true, Orlov," nodded Rupert. "On the other hand, once we have them, we can restore your beauty."

"Good!" said Orlov, huffily, and he sat back in his seat and sulked for a time.

"How do we know that this second dagger even

exists?" asked Inspector Klaw, who hadn't been so eager to join the party going to England. He had hoped that the vampire scourge was behind him for ever. Then his chief, to his utter surprise, had said it was a good idea, as it might put an end to the vampire "nonsense", as he called it, for good. "I know you have read about it, Professor," continued Klaw. "That you have some interesting notes by the designer of the dagger, the blind monk called Marvin, and Helsing has heard of its existence from years gone by. But that was all *then*. What *now*? It might be destroyed, or lie rusting at the bottom of the River Thames."

"It cannot be destroyed, and it cannot rust," said Helsing in a level voice. "You must accept that as fact. As for finding it," he said, shaking his head. "It will be difficult. But I know that Dracula has sent agents to London in search of it. That he has several agents working for him all over the city. He must know *some*thing of the matter to have begun such a thorough search. He wouldn't waste his time on a wild goose chase."

"Any other proof?" asked Klaw.

"There *is* something else," interrupted the professor. All eyes switched to him. "Have you noticed how silent Dracula has been in recent years? Not a hint of trouble has come out of Castle Bran. Why would that be? His whole existence is littered with death and destruction."

"So, what are you saying, Professor?" asked Rupert.

"That Dracula has been waiting for the moment when he could be sure he had traced the second dagger."

"I know one other thing," added Helsing. "One of the agents he is using is Rupert's father, Count Arnold Krinkelfiend."

"Father!" gasped Rupert. "You never mentioned it before!" he said.

"It was something I wanted to keep to myself until I was certain," Helsing explained. "But now that the inspector is pressing for an answer, and we are all sat here considering the situation. . ."

"But how do you know Father is involved?" asked Rupert, leaning forward.

"I, too, have agents." Helsing smiled. "Remember, I am Dracula's worst enemy."

"Well, I guess it's good we know what we're up against in advance," sighed Rupert. "No doubt Father will try to give us a warm welcome in London."

"Like the one he gave us in Bran that time, when he burst into the cathedral on a stallion," remembered Klaw with a shudder.

"Yes, Father can be quite a nuisance on occasion," nodded Rupert.

"Keep your voices down," grumbled Orlov.

"You're not *still* in a bad mood," sighed Rupert.

Orlov wasn't in a bad mood. Orlov had seen something. He touched his twisted lips with a finger indicating they should be silent. Then he pointed one of his many deformed fingers at the carriage door window which looked on to the corridor. Helsing slowly peered around the frame until he could see.

"There's nothing there, Orlov," he whispered.

"Perhaps not," said Orlov, "but there *was* something there. A some*one* in fact. And he was listening in."

"Would you recognize him again?" asked Helsing.

"Oh, yes," chuckled Orlov, in a gravelly voice.

"It's easy to recognize a bristly, fat man supported by not one, but *two* wooden legs."

They all exchanged concerned looks. "If our arrival in England is known so soon," said Rupert, "then we must be on our guard from the moment we get to London."

No one disagreed.

The intrepid team had left their train at Waterloo station, and were travelling in a hansom cab towards a small hotel…

❦ Chapter Three
London by Night

Percy Picklewhite showed Sergeant Probe his office. "And this is the room you left the coffin in, sir?" said the sergeant.

"Yes, Sergeant," said an anxious Picklewhite. "And . . . and the delivery people said there was a *body* in it."

"I see, sir," frowned the sergeant. "Though how would they know that, sir?"

Picklewhite threw his hands in the air. "*I* don't know," he said. "Maybe they were just fooling around."

"Hmm."

The sergeant moved awkwardly from one foot to the other. "I don't like to accuse anyone of wasting police time, sir," he said finally, "but we made some enquiries back at the station. The thing is, sir, the delivery company have no record of having delivered a coffin to this address. Indeed, they laughed and told me they have never delivered a coffin anywhere in their fifteen years of service."

"Impossible!" cried Picklewhite. "Look, I can prove it. I put a copy of the receipt they made me sign here on my desk."

Picklewhite went to his desk and began searching frantically beneath bundles of papers and documents. "It *has* to be here somewhere."

But it wasn't. Picklewhite, of course, wasn't to know that Dracula's two employees were not *real* delivery people, and that the receipt had been pocketed by the artful Count Krinkelfiend.

"Very good, sir," said the sergeant. "We'll ignore

the matter this time, but please have more solid evidence should such a matter occur again."

The sergeant left. Percy Picklewhite collapsed on his desk and began sobbing. "I'm going to have a long holiday," he said aloud to the empty room. "Yes, that's what I need. I've been working too hard. That must be it."

"London's very foggy," complained Orlov. "I can't see *any*thing!"

The intrepid team had left their train at Waterloo station, and were travelling in a hansom cab towards a small hotel that Helsing had booked.

"London is *always* foggy," said the professor. "You will grow used to it, my boy."

The wooden wheels of the cab clattered noisily over the smooth cobbled streets.

"I still don't see how we are going to track down a single dagger in a city so big," said Inspector Klaw.

"*And* so foggy!" added Orlov.

"We need to find Krinkelfiend, I imagine," said Helsing. "*He* must know something, if he's here on Dracula's behest."

23

"Follow Father?" said Rupert. "That might be a little dangerous, if not a little difficult. Father can be somewhat elusive when he wishes to be."

"But you have your old vampire powers back," Helsing reminded him. "Krinkelfiend might not be expecting that. You will be able to do things unseen."

Rupert nodded thoughtfully. "It is true my powers are greater than they've been in years. I can turn things into any shape I wish."

"Then turn me into a handsome prince," grumbled Orlov.

"There are limits to my powers, Orlov," frowned Rupert.

As their cab rumbled onwards, another carriage followed close behind in the murky night-time London streets.

"Well, this is a bit of fun," said Itch, from inside the pursuing cab. "It's good to get out and about a bit."

"So long as we don't get caught," said Scratch, who had hoped their days working for Vermyn were behind them.

"You will be fine," said Vermyn, who was sat

opposite them. "Just don't get careless like you did that last time in Grund."

"It's busier here," said Itch. "Easier to hide among all the citizens."

"And foggy, too," agreed Scratch. "Easier to lose anyone following us."

"Good conditions for robbing people, wouldn't you say, big brother?"

"Excellent, little brother."

"Keep your minds on the job in hand," cautioned Vermyn. "My employer is paying you well for your full cooperation. Remember that."

"And how is that old vampire count of yours these days?" asked Scratch. "Got bored with hiding in Silver Valley, did he?"

"Don't refer to him in such a way," warned Vermyn. "He senses everything."

"I've always wondered," said Itch. "Does he have sharp teeth?"

"Be useful to have sharp teeth," said Scratch. "You can eat things easily with sharp teeth."

"Wouldn't need a knife and fork with sharp teeth," said Itch.

"You don't use a knife and fork anyway," Scratch told him.

"No. But if I did and I had sharp teeth," said Itch, "I wouldn't need to, would I?"

Vermyn, who was still grinning, but only just, shook his head in despair. Working with these brothers again was like reliving an old nightmare.

"Hey, look!" said Scratch. "Their cab's pulled up outside that hotel."

"Good," said Vermyn, who was tiring of playing detective. He had first observed Helsing and his colleagues aboard the ship that had brought him to Portsmouth, and had been tracking their movements ever since. Much to Itch and Scratch's irritation, it had meant that they had had to spend most of the voyage locked in their cabins to avoid recognition.

"We'll tell our driver to pull up as well, and you two can follow them into the hotel. Only don't be seen by them. Be cautious at all times."

"I could do with something to eat," said Itch. "All that talk of sharp teeth has made me hungry."

"And so you shall, little brother," said Scratch,

"once we've booked ourselves into a cosy room, we'll get room service to bring us two fat, juicy steaks."

Vermyn left the brothers there, and took another hansom cab further into the city towards the Thames. He had a rendezvous to keep.

Eventually, he reached his destination. "Just here please, cabbie," he told the driver. Climbing softly down from the cab, he paid the driver, and moved hurriedly through the foggy darkness.

"Strange place for a well-dressed gentleman to want to come at this time of night," thought the cabbie, as he pulled away.

Vermyn passed a noisy tavern, where light flooded on to the street and drunken customers were singing popular songs of the day. Then he found the address he was searching for – 12 Derry Street. A grim location, but then vampires, he knew, preferred grim locations.

He was about to knock on the door, but it opened before he had a chance.

"Are you Vermyn?" asked a big, bristly faced man with two wooden legs. Vermyn gulped nervously. He thought Itch and Scratch were bad enough.

"Er, yes," he replied quietly. "I've come to see. . ."

The wooden-legged man heaved him inside and slammed the door.

Vermyn found himself inside a small but decorative hallway.

"I am Grog!" he told him.

"Pleased to meet you, I'm sure," grinned Vermyn.

His wooden legs clacked noisily across the flagstone floor, as he led Vermyn to another door. There, Grog knocked once.

"Come!" beckoned a muffled voice from within. But it was a familiar voice to Vermyn.

"In you go!" ordered Grog, eyeing Vermyn suspiciously.

"Er, thank you, er, Grog."

The room Vermyn entered was very dark. Count Arnold Krinkelfiend was sitting in an armchair in what, to Vermyn's surprise, was a pleasant and normal drawing room. After his experiences of the count's lair in Silver Valley, almost anything was pleasant and normal.

"Your mighty countship," bowed Vermyn, with grin locked firmly in place.

"How are you enjoying your freedom?" asked Krinkelfiend.

"Very, very much, oh merciful Count," cringed Vermyn. "You spared me from a miserable time in my life."

"Good. And the reason I did so is the second dagger," said Krinkelfiend, getting straight to business. "Have you formulated a plan yet? My *own* master has high expectations. It would not do for us to fail in our quest."

"Yes, indeed, your countship," grinned Vermyn. "I have men working on the situation as we speak."

"This is encouraging," nodded Krinkelfiend. "And?"

"Well, it is very early days, of course –" Vermyn shuffled like a long snake – "we having only just arrived in London. But the way I see it, is this dagger was last observed in a display of artefacts at the British Museum. This was some time ago, I believe, but there is no reason it should not still be there."

"That is believed to be the case," said Krinkelfiend, forming a steeple with his hands.

"Then I must arrange its removal."

"You will be caught," said Krinkelfiend, very matter-of-factly.

"Oh no, my count," said Vermyn, with mock surprise at such doubt. "Stealing is an art in which I am well-versed."

After a moment of thought, Krinkelfiend slowly nodded. "I am pleased to hear it," he said finally. "I have clearly employed the right gentleman for this task. The mistakes of the past might not have been solely yours."

"Oh thank you, your countship."

"However, it is a task I would have preferred to carry out alone," said Krinkelfiend. "My night vision and skills of transformation are very useful for such occasions."

"Of course, your countship."

"But I see myself as important to my master, and therefore should not endanger myself, or attract undue attention."

"In other words," thought Vermyn, "he wants me to take the blame should anything go wrong!"

"And Grog will always be nearby should you need any back-up," added Krinkelfiend.

"Most reassuring to know that," grinned Vermyn, while thinking that Grog's noisy wooden legs could give the game away in no time, and ruin all his plans for a successful theft. "Might I just request, with your kind permission, Count," said Vermyn, choosing his words carefully, "that you allow me to work alone. At least, that is, for twenty-four hours. You see, I work so much better alone, though I can see Grog's talents are enormous. . ."

"You may have twenty-four hours," agreed Krinkelfiend. "No longer, as I sense danger. We know my former son and his foolish friends are on the scent of the dagger. It won't take them long to track it down to the British Museum."

"I'll beat them to it, your countship," promised Vermyn.

"You had better," threatened Krinkelfiend. "Now leave me."

Vermyn fell out on to the foggy street again. He felt cold, but it wasn't the weather. It was a coldness deep within that he always felt after his interviews with the vampire.

"Are you sure you're not wearing mine?" said Scratch.

✒ Chapter Four
The Search Begins

The following morning, Helsing and his colleagues visited the British Museum. Orlov wore a hooded cloak to disguise his face, which would have caused unwanted attention if exposed. "Are we really likely to find the dagger on display here?" asked Inspector Klaw, somewhat sceptical of the idea.

"Like Dracula, I too have a certain ability to sense

things, Inspector," said Helsing. "And right now, my senses are telling me that the dagger has definitely been inside this building. Therefore, it makes a good starting point. A *very* good starting point."

"If the second dagger is in London," explained the professor, "it will either be privately owned, or on display. The British Museum has some of the finest displays of such artefacts. So Herr Helsing's senses are likely to be proved right, Inspector."

"I stand corrected," shrugged Inspector Klaw.

"Or it could be in an attic, a cupboard, a box, a dustbin. . ." suggested Orlov.

"It's rare I find myself saying it," said Klaw, not understanding how Helsing could sense the presence of an ancient dagger, "but I agree with Orlov. The places the dagger could be are endless."

"Not so," said Helsing. "You see, the dagger is a magical object. The remarkable blind monk, Marvin, was a unique person; as unique as Dracula, in his own way. This isn't just an exotic dagger we are talking about, Inspector; it is an amazing object. As amazing as the first we came across. Marvin has made these daggers amazing.

Neither dagger would allow itself to be discarded. Even the first dagger, you will recall, was on display at Viktoria Palace for centuries."

"Yes," nodded Klaw. "King Konstantine and Princess Lashka owned it."

"And other kings and queens long before *them*," said Helsing. Then he smiled. "I don't think anyone really *owns* these daggers," he said. "These daggers are virtually alive."

Klaw shuddered at the thought.

"At least there's no fog in here," observed Orlov, as they walked slowly through the giant, marble building, every sound bouncing off the tall walls and ceiling.

"It is important to remember that the daggers are a pair," said Rupert. "They need each other to be complete. It was never Marvin or Dracula's intention that they should be separated. Although we know little of them, we can be certain their forces will work to rejoin. We saw that there were limitations with the first dagger, when kept on its own. It is the combining of the two that we are here to prevent."

"But can we?" said Klaw, who was beginning to miss the more simple life of Gertcha.

"I imagine Dracula will be making sure places such as these are being searched thoroughly," said the professor. "He might even have someone here this very minute."

"To be sure whether it is or is not here," said Helsing, "or that it was *once* here, but is no longer, we must find where the records of all items entering this place are kept."

"That was my intention from the moment you suggested coming here, Helsing," said Rupert.

Everyone looked at him. "Well, it's simple for me, isn't it?" he shrugged. "When the place closes this evening, I remain behind. Then I've got all night to hunt around."

"That makes sense," agreed Helsing.

"You'll never get away with it," scorned Orlov.

"You forget, Orlov, that my powers are much improved. I can cloak myself into any inanimate object in this building. A chair, a picture, a table. . ."

"How about a handsome prince?"

"Enough about that, Orlov," sighed Rupert.

"If you help rather than hinder, we'll have the dagger all the sooner and you will have your good looks."

A vague glow came over Orlov. The idea of being strong and handsome again often overwhelmed him these days.

"It's just Father I must watch out for," Rupert continued. "Father, and anyone he's employed to do his dirty work."

"Talking of which," said Klaw, his eyes suddenly ablaze. "I *know* that man over there." He pointed at a tall, grinning man, who was making great pretence of interest in a Ming vase.

"Who is he?" asked Helsing in a whisper.

"Vermyn!" spat Klaw. "A miserable character who has made a career of working for the likes of Count Krinkelfiend. I arrested him over the Viktoria Palace episode. He's supposed to be serving a long jail sentence. It would appear that he is well-acquainted with Count Krinkelfiend."

"Presumably, Father decided he had been in prison long enough," said Rupert.

"I wonder what *his* plan is. . .?" said Helsing.

After a bad night spent listening to Itch and Scratch snoring and sleeptalking, Vermyn had breakfasted then made straight for the British Museum, as per his instructions. If the dagger was there, and it was supposed to be, he would choose his moment carefully then steal it. But he had soon discovered just how large the museum was, and how many guards hovered about the place.

"Only one thing for it," he thought. "I'll stay here after closing this evening. Then I'll steal it during the dead of night." He chuckled inwardly. "No one will see me if I'm careful." A wide, irrepressible grin was fixed to his face. "It will be easy at night. Then, with the coming of morning, I will mingle with the visitors and disappear with the dagger. What happy days these are."

"This is Hyde Park," said Scratch.

"How do you know?" said Itch.

"Vermyn said it was the only park in this direction."

"And Vermyn knows everything."

"So he thinks," chuckled Scratch.

"Well, he knows how to pay," said Itch, and his smile revealed rotten gums and wobbly black teeth.

"So tell me, big brother," said Itch, "what are we doing in Hyde Park. Hiding?"

"Good one, little brother," chortled Scratch. "What we're doing, is watching."

"Watching what?"

"Watching out for the enemy."

"What, Klaw and all that lot?" said Itch. "I thought they were in Gertcha."

"No one is sure," said Scratch. "That's why we're being paid to keep a look out."

"If I bump into that Klaw, he'll regret it," said Itch, meaningfully. "Got us put away, he did."

"That's his job," said Scratch. "We're the criminals, and he's the law. You can't have one without the other."

"I hadn't thought about it that way before," said Itch.

A well-dressed gentleman and lady passed by them. "Look at all of them in this park," said Itch. "Dead smart in all their refinery."

"Yes, and look at us!" snarled Scratch. "We look like tramps."

"We don't have to."

"Eh?"

"We've had our first payment," said Itch. "Let's smarten ourselves up. Look the part."

An hour later, Itch and Scratch found themselves strolling in Hyde Park again. This time, they were dressed in smart suits. Smart suits that didn't quite fit.

"Are you sure you're not wearing mine?" said Scratch.

"They're very uncomfortable," complained Itch.

Itch looked at his brother and laughed. "You look like an undertaker!"

"And you look like the body he's just buried!" retorted Scratch.

"C'mon, big brother," said Itch. "Let's rest our legs on that bench over there. We're not going to bump into Klaw and his friends in a place as big as London."

The two men sat down and watched the elegant citizens of London glide by.

"Well, we certainly don't look quite like *that* lot," observed Itch.

"We blend in better than we did, though," said Scratch.

"Even bought myself a newspaper to look the part," said Itch. "Wonder if it's got any nice pictures in it!"

"It better have," chuckled Scratch. "You can't even read your *own* language, let alone English!"

Itch began to while away the minutes flicking through page after page of newsprint and illustration.

"Hey, look!" he suddenly said.

"Good pictures, then?" teased Scratch. "Seen a nice mansion you might want to buy?"

"Look here!" said Itch, excitedly.

"What now?"

"It's an illustration," said Itch, showing him.

Scratch studied the picture for a moment. "Yes, you're right. It's an illustration of a knife. So what?"

"Not a knife, big brother. A dagger!"

Scratch looked again. "So, it's a dagger. So what?"

"And what is it Vermyn's looking for?"

"Yes, yes, yes. Vermyn's looking for a dagger," said Scratch irritably, "but why should an

41

illustration of a dagger in a daily newspaper be *the* dagger that grinning idiot's after?"

"I dunno! Just a thought," said Itch, and he tossed the paper on the ground.

"On the other hand. . ." Scratch dived to the ground and retrieved the paper, getting some odd looks from the rather pompous people walking past their bench.

"What is it?" said Itch excitedly. "Have I done something useful?"

"You might have, little brother, you might have."

Scratch turned to the page again. "There!" he said. "The dagger in the illustration is resting on something."

"Yes, a velvet cloth of some kind," said Itch. "What's your point?"

"Turn your beady little eyes to the corner of the cloth," said Scratch. "Can you see the emblem?"

"Wow! A symbol of some kind. Looks like a shield."

"It is," said Scratch. "It's a *Romanian* shield.

"So it is."

Scratch folded the paper and shoved it roughly

into the pocket of his new jacket. "I think old misery guts might be interested in this, don't you?"

"Could be worth an extra kronk or two," sniggered Itch.

"C'mon," said Scratch. "Let's get out of here!"

Dermyn's grin at once returned to its fullest.
"So, you are Rupert, the count's discarded son."

✦ Chapter Five
When Rupert met Vermyn

The public shuffled out of the large museum into the last of the daylight. Everyone, that is, except Rupert, who hid behind one of the tall columns that ran from the floor to the high ceiling. And there he waited.

The clinking and clanking of locking doors eventually stopped. All Rupert could hear were the sharp footfalls of a security guard bouncing around the large building. They never stopped, because the guard spent the night examining every inch of the dark building, a lantern in hand, illuminating his path.

Rupert clicked his fingers and, in a puff of purple smoke, he reappeared in bat form. He flew towards the ceiling, where he could get a better view. Far beneath him, he could see the flickering yellow light of the guard's lantern. His night vision was excellent, which is how he soon noticed a *second* shadowy figure moving around the building.

"Another guard?" he wondered. "Doubtful! He doesn't make any noise."

Rupert swooped lower, in and out of the tall support columns. If he hadn't been on such an important mission, he would have quite enjoyed his aerial antics.

"That's no guard, all right!" he thought, swooping ever closer to Vermyn. "He's trying not to be seen, too. It looks like that Vermyn fellow, whom the inspector spotted earlier on."

Vermyn grinned his wide and senseless grin. Happy to have eluded the museum's security, he carefully skirted the ground floor, found the main stairwell, and skipped silently up to the first floor.

"Ah!" thought Vermyn. "And there is the office of the museum. Just the place where the records on items stored and displayed in this vast building will be kept."

He pulled a bunch of skeleton keys from his pocket – keys that could undo almost any lock known to man – and moved cautiously forward towards the door. Suddenly he stopped, aware that something was fluttering close to his face.

"Get away!" he said, swiping out in the dimness.

With another puff of purple smoke, Rupert stood before him, blocking his path to the office door.

"Count Krinkelfiend!" gasped Vermyn, momentarily confused.

"Almost," smiled Rupert. "Try adding 'junior'."

Vermyn's grin at once returned to its fullest. "So, you are Rupert, the count's discarded son," he said with scorn. "How disappointed he must be in you."

"My family affairs are my *own* business," said Rupert, folding his arms.

47

"Does your daddy know you are out at this time of night?" Vermyn continued to mock Rupert.

"Look here, Vermyn – yes, I know who you are, too. I can turn you into a slab of stone if I so choose, so don't irritate me."

"I see," said Vermyn, in a low, gravelly voice. "So, suddenly we have magic powers, do we? That's not what *I* had heard. Maybe you're expecting me to burst into tears and run screaming from the building?" His grin became more menacing. "Or maybe I should stop listening to your nonsense and toss you off the nearest balcony to the ground floor."

"I wouldn't advise trying it, if I were you," Rupert warned him.

"WHO GOES THERE?"

The sound of the security guard's voice made both men turn to the stairwell.

"I'M ARMED WITH A TRUNCHEON," warned the guard, "AND I'M NOT AFRAID TO USE IT!"

They could hear his footsteps coming closer and closer.

The guard soon reached the office. Nothing

appeared out of place – except, perhaps, the strange stone statue near the office door. "That's not from the museum," thought the guard, scratching the back of his head. "We don't *keep* any statues of men in modern dress. Especially ones with a huge grin on their face!"

Rupert returned to the hotel. "A great shame, my boy," said the professor, consolingly. "Still, at least it proves that Dracula expects to find his second dagger there."

"I turned Vermyn into stone," explained Rupert. "He really is the most obnoxious man you could imagine. It served him right."

"I'm sure it did," said Helsing, with a smile.

"It's only a mild spell," said Rupert. "It shouldn't last more than a couple of hours. I doubt he'll dare hang around the place once he's back to normal."

"I wonder if he's working alone," said Inspector Klaw. "Last time I crossed his path, he employed the Ripaka brothers. And they're as irritating as Vermyn himself."

"I want to go home," groaned Orlov. "We're never going to get this dagger."

"We will go home soon," promised Rupert. "But firstly, I must return to the museum. Guard or no guard, I must track down the dagger. If I don't, then Dracula's men surely will. And that would not be very good for anyone."

"That might not be necessary," said the professor, suddenly.

All eyes turned to him.

"I was just flicking through the pages of this magazine I found in the lobby," he explained.

"Go on, Professor," urged Helsing.

"Well, I shall read out the words that accompany an illustration of a very familiar dagger. 'Items from the Estate of the late Mister Smallbone will be auctioned on October 22nd.' That's tomorrow, gentlemen," the professor pointed out. " 'Among these items are many valuable works of art and artefacts, including a Romanian dagger and sheath with original velvet pouch.' "

"Well, well, well," sighed Rupert. "*That* changes things a bit. And the sale is tomorrow?"

"At eleven in the morning," confirmed the professor. "We must hope our enemies know nothing of this matter."

"So, the second dagger must have been privately purchased by this Mister Smallbone from the British Museum," said Inspector Klaw, thinking it through. "And then he died, leaving the dagger with all the rest of the stuff that makes up his estate."

"We must bid whatever it takes to get the dagger," said Rupert. "Money is not a problem when you can apply a little vampire magic."

"That's all very well," said Orlov, unconvinced, "but it doesn't actually say, 'including a Romanian dagger made by Marvin, the blind monk, for Count Dracula', does it?"

"Well, obviously it doesn't," said Rupert. "Only *we* know all about such matters."

"You have seen the first dagger, Orlov," said the professor. "Come here and look at this illustration."

Orlov trundled awkwardly over to the professor and glanced down upon the illustration. His doubt lifted from his face. "That is it!" he gasped. "That is the dagger that will help make me beautiful again.

I could never forget its . . . its beauty."

"And look," said Helsing, coming up behind them. "On the velvet pouch is a Romanian shield." He exchanged a knowing look with the professor. "The shield is of a specific family. The Basarab family!"

"Count Vlad Dracula's line!" said the Professor, in a subdued, reverent voice. After a silent pause, he leapt to his feet. "How exciting this all is!"

"One of us must attend the auction tomorrow," said Helsing. He glanced at the magazine again. "It's in Mayfair, near Park Lane."

"Who is the least conspicuous?" asked Klaw.

"*I* could go," suggested Orlov, eager to see, to touch, to hold the real dagger.

"Out of the question, Orlov," said Helsing. "You look too . . . too. . ."

"Too ugly! I know that's what you mean," said Orlov. "Too hideous, too frightening. Little children will scream and run when they catch sight of the deformed Orlov; his grotesque body, his deformed. . ."

"Be quiet, Orlov," said Rupert gently. Then he

turned to his friends. "However, gentlemen: on this occasion, Orlov is right."

Everyone looked at him as if he were mad. "I *am*?" said Orlov, equally as confused.

"All of us are very recognizable to the opposition – except for Orlov."

Orlov smiled happily, his lips parting like two ripe bananas being prised apart.

"If Vermyn appears at this private auction tomorrow, he will recognize the policeman who had him put away. He will recognize me, the son of Count Krinkelfiend, who confronted him in the museum. He will recognize Helsing, because *every*one involved with the daggers will by now know Helsing. And the professor. . ." he concluded with a smile. "Dracula, Father, Vermyn . . . they all know you, Professor. And, if I might say so, you do look like a professor."

"Thank you – I *think*," said the professor.

"But Orlov," mused Rupert. "He only returned when Dracula returned. He then became handsome."

"Ooh yes – so very handsome," remembered Orlov.

"So, I think we might get away with sending Orlov – a hooded, slightly disguised Orlov."

"Yes," nodded Helsing. "They might take him for an eccentric wealthy foreigner."

"That sounds nice." Orlov grinned hideously.

"Will the dagger allow itself to be taken away?" said the professor.

"It has clearly not been within Dracula's powers yet," said Rupert, "or it would already be in his possession like the first dagger. No," he decided, "the dagger will let us do anything for the time being, just as it has done for the British Museum, and later, the private owner – this poor deceased Mister Smallbone."

"Well, *I'm* up for giving it a try," said Orlov. "I'll do anything to be beautiful again."

"Yes, we gathered that, Orlov," said Rupert, and everyone – including Orlov – laughed.

The tavern on the banks of the River Thames was filled with dark corners and clouds of smoke from pipe-smoking sailors just arrived from India on the nearby wharf.

"Despite passing a miserable evening as a stone statue inside the British Museum," said Vermyn, "I have actually ended my day on a very happy note because of the two of you."

Itch and Scratch chuckled merrily at that. A happy Vermyn always meant a fistful of kronks in their hands.

"Glad to have been of service," said Scratch.

"Yes, you can always rely on us," smiled Itch.

"This illustration," said Vermyn, leering over the magazine, and tapping the drawing of the dagger with a pointed finger, "is the key to all our problems."

"I told you it was worth following up," said Scratch to Itch.

"It was *me* who found it," complained Itch.

"But me who did something about it, eh?"

"Enough!" signalled Vermyn. "Before I report these findings to my employer, we need to decide which of us is going to attend tomorrow's auction at –" he glanced at the words on the page – ". . .at Mayfair."

"Maybe we should *all* go," suggested Scratch.

"Yes," said Itch. "We could be your back-up."

"I think not," grinned Vermyn. "I am more known than either of you two." What he meant, of course, was if there was to be any trouble, he didn't want a part of it. "I think it best you go alone. Bid what is necessary to buy the dagger – I imagine it will reach a fairly high price – then return to our hotel room. Got that?"

"Nothing could be easier," said Scratch.

"I agree," smiled Itch. "Nothing easier."

"Then the matter is settled," grinned Vermyn.

"It is?" said Itch.

"It might be dangerous," said Scratch, suddenly thinking a bit more about what they'd just agreed to do.

"*Very* dangerous, big brother," agreed Itch, his smile fading.

"You will be well rewarded," promised Vermyn. "*Extremely* well rewarded."

"Like we always say," smiled Itch, and Scratch was smiling too. "Where there's a kronk there's a way!"

"Excellent, gentlemen," grinned Vermyn. "And

now, for the next few hours, I am going to teach you English numerals. It might give you the edge when it comes to bidding for the dagger."

"Oh," sighed Itch. "It's like being back at school."

"We never *went* to school," said Scratch.

"No, but if we had, it would feel like we were back at it!"

Vermyn took a deep breath. It was going to be a long night. . .

"*Oh my goodness,*" *said the man to Orlov. "You have*
twenty fingers!" Then he promptly fainted.

⚘ Chapter Six
A Battle of Wits

Whispers went around the Mayfair home of the late Mister Smallbone when Orlov stepped into the room.

"He might be wearing a hood," said one voice, "but what a face lies beneath it!"

"Poor creature!"

"Maybe he's one of those eccentric foreign millionaires we hear so much about."

And there were other, less flattering comments.

Orlov ignored it all. He had an important job to do; one that could leave him the most handsome person in the whole of the world. *Then* they wouldn't say nasty things behind his back!

Orlov took a seat at the rear of the room, which wasn't a seat at all, but Rupert – who had *cloaked* himself into a seat. Soon after, the auction was under way.

Rupert's promise of an endless supply of money – albeit *fake* money – which Orlov could use to bid for the second dagger left the deformed former servant to Dracula feeling quite calm. He knew, through Rupert's magic, he could outbid anyone in the room.

Many items came and went, and Orlov yawned as yet another table, desk, chair, painting came under the auctioneer's hammer.

"And now," said the auctioneer finally, "we come to lot number 22. A beautiful, handcrafted, bejewelled dagger of Romanian origin. What am I bid? Shall we start at one thousand pounds?"

"YES!" shouted Orlov, not actually understanding what the man was saying, but knowing he was talking about the dagger.

The auctioneer frowned. "Any advance on one thousand pounds?"

"Two thousand!" said a voice at the front.

Now it was Orlov's turn to frown.

"Any advance on two?" said the auctioneer. "Do I hear two thousand five hundred?"

"YES!" called Orlov again, hoping it was the appropriate moment to call out.

"Er, very good, sir," said the auctioneer, giving Orlov a glare. "Do I hear. . .?"

"Four thousand pounds!" said the voice at the front.

"That was a bit steep," Itch told his bidding brother.

"It'll get rid of the competition," Scratch whispered.

A tiny ripple of excitement passed through the room. The dozens gathered could tell this was turning into a battle between two wealthy and determined bidders.

"The gentleman at the back of the room," said the auctioneer. "I see your hand raised, sir. What are you bidding against four thousand pounds?"

"YES!" said Orlov, using his one word of English again. Everyone in the room chuckled.

"I need a figure, sir," pressed the auctioneer,

raising his hammer, keen to end this nonsense.

Everyone waited on the hooded foreigner. "Perhaps four thousand five hundred?" assisted the auctioneer.

"YES!" called Orlov.

"Five thousand!" said Scratch at once.

The ripple of interest was growing rapidly. Even with all the jewels, this old dagger surely wasn't worth the king's ransom being offered.

Orlov could tell he was being outbid. He turned to the man next to him and showed him both hands with ten fingers on each.

"How many's that?" Orlov asked him.

"I'm sorry, sir, I do not understand your tongue."

Orlov held his hands closer to the man's face.

Meanwhile, the auctioneer was raising his hammer to bring proceedings to a close. "Are we done, ladies and gentlemen?" he said. "Going once, going twice. . ."

"Oh my goodness," said the man to Orlov. "You have twenty fingers!" Then he promptly fainted.

"TWENTY!" Orlov shouted back at the auctioneer.

The room became raucous.

"WHAT?" gasped Scratch.

"We're being pummelled," said Itch. "Vermyn never told us it would go for anything *like* that much."

"Er, twenty thousand pounds?" checked the auctioneer, loosening his tie and collar.

"YES!" called Orlov, thinking, "What does he keep saying to me, I wonder!"

"Going once, going twice, gone to the man in the hood at the back of the room," said the auctioneer, and the hammer cracked down on the table, bringing the bidding to a close.

"Beaten at the post!" cried Scratch.

"Vermyn will murder us!" sobbed Itch.

"Well done, Orlov," whispered Orlov's chair. "You *are* rather heavy, though. Could you get off me now?"

"Oh, right," said Orlov, standing.

"Bravo, sir!" said a few people in Orlov's vicinity, and he could tell by their happy smiles and the pats on his back that he had done well.

Orlov and the purchasers of other items were shown into an adjoining room.

"Your dagger, sir," said one of the auctioneer's men, passing it to him.

"Thanks!" said Orlov, using the only other word he knew in English apart from "yes".

"And how would sir like to pay?"

"Yes!" said Orlov.

"Er, does that mean cash or cheque, sir?"

"Yes!"

Then Orlov glanced down at his malformed hand, and as if by magic – which it was – there was exactly twenty thousand pounds in it.

"In cash, sir!" beamed the assistant, also noticing the notes. "Most civilized, sir."

They exchanged money for dagger and Orlov, smiling beneath his hood, made to leave.

Itch and Scratch, however, blocked his path. "Look," said Scratch in a low voice. "We don't have the cash with us, but we know a man who'll pay you double if you give it over!"

"I don't *want* double," said Orlov, clasping tightly to the dagger. "It's the dagger, I want. And I've got it, so there!" Then Orlov added, suddenly suspicious, "How come you can speak Romanian?"

"Who are you, ugly stranger?" asked Itch.

"You should know," said Orlov. "He came with you!"

"Not him, you fool," said Itch. "I mean who are *you*?"

"Oh, right," said Orlov. "I'm the one who's just got himself a very nice dagger. Goodbye, gentlemen."

"Grab him!" called Scratch, as Orlov made to scarper.

"I . . . I can't move my legs!" said Itch.

"Me neither!" cried Scratch. "What's going on here? Hey, you! Ugly one! We have friends in high places."

"And I have friends in lots of places," the retreating Orlov called back.

"I did it, I did it!" cried Orlov to Rupert, who was waiting for him outside.

"Steady, Orlov," said Rupert. "A little dignity, please. Wealthy buyers don't behave like that."

"Oh, right!"

"Saw those two idiots confront you so I put a short-term spell on them. It'll give us long enough to get back to the hotel."

"Good," said Orlov. Then he grinned. "They'll be 'stuck' here some time, then?"

"Come on, Orlov," sighed Rupert. "Let's get back to the others."

Grog was soon trundling clumsily down the corridor on his wooden legs.

◆ Chapter Seven
Joy Short-lived

That night, Count Krinkelfiend, in bat form, left his secret London address, and flew over the murky London rooftops, keeping close to the snaking path of the River Thames, which sparkled in the glow of the moon.

He landed, with a splat, in front of a small hut on the muddy banks of the river. "I'm beginning to dislike this country!" he said aloud.

"Ah, your countship," beamed Vermyn, trudging through the mud to meet him.

"This isn't the most comfortable of addresses for us to meet again, Vermyn," snarled Krinkelfiend.

"I apologize, Count, for these inhospitable circumstances," said Vermyn. "But all will soon be well."

Krinkelfiend perked up. "You have the second dagger?"

"*Almost*, your countship."

"Only *almost*!" said Krinkelfiend, his voice developing a dangerous edge, and his hands beginning to reach out to Vermyn's throat.

"I know exactly where it is, Count," blurted Vermyn.

"You do? Then what is the problem?"

"We require a bit of your . . . your wonderful magic, oh great Count."

Krinkelfiend was not against a bit of showing off; especially if it was he who was doing the showing off.

"What exactly do you require?" he asked him.

"Well, Count, the enemy have the dagger in a hotel. Your son. . ."

"My *former* son," corrected Krinkelfiend. "I knew he would have to meddle in this. Next time he and I meet, I will transform him into something so unpleasant that all other unpleasant things won't seem that unpleasant after all."

"Yes, quite, your countship," grinned Vermyn. "Your *former* son," he corrected himself, "is with the enemy. He proved to me he has some powers . . . not *great* powers such as yours, mighty Count, but dangerous to a mortal such as myself. If you were to give me or one of my associates some protection. . .?" He let the sentence trail away.

"I promised my master we would avoid personal confrontation," said Krinkelfiend. "However. . ." and a little wily grin appeared on his thin, bloodless lips. "I think that Grog will enjoy the work."

"As you wish, sir," bowed Vermyn. "Do you think he can manage? Alone, I mean?"

"I will give him the protection he requires," said Krinkelfiend. "And Grog is familiar with London. He's the best agent for this task."

"An excellent idea, Count," grovelled Vermyn, "and soon the dagger will be in your grasp."

"It had better be, Vermyn," warned Krinkelfiend. "If not, your neck will be!"

Vermyn gulped.

"Prepare our passage for Transylvania. We leave on the first boat tomorrow. And we'll be taking a dagger with us."

Krinkelfiend burst into maniacal laughter, exploded into a bat and took to the night sky.

Helsing and his colleagues examined the dagger in the safety of their hotel room.

"Quite remarkable;" observed Professor von Morcumstein. "You did well, Orlov."

Orlov blushed, but whenever he did so, he tended to turn green.

"They appeared to think he was an eccentric millionaire," chuckled Rupert.

Helsing seemed unwilling to join in the fun of the moment. "You seem distracted, old friend?" Rupert said.

"Oh, it is nothing," said Helsing. "It's good we have managed to achieve in London what we set out to achieve."

"But?" prompted the professor.

"But we are still only the carriers of the dagger," said Helsing. "We have yet to escape London and return home. And then there's the spell you made to create the false money."

"It was necessary," said Rupert. "Without it we would not be admiring the second dagger."

"Yes, I fully agree," said Helsing.

"It's the repercussions you fear," said Inspector Klaw, recognizing the problem.

"Yes, Inspector," nodded Helsing.

"Once the spell wears off," said Klaw, "the police will be alerted. A trace will be put out on Orlov. And Orlov, if he'll forgive me, isn't the hardest person to miss."

"I'll forgive you," smiled Orlov, who was willing to forgive anything now they had the second dagger.

"All we need do is get on the first ship leaving these shores tomorrow," assured Rupert. "We'll have enough problems to deal with back in the homeland. For a start, we must work out what to do with the dagger to prevent Dracula retrieving it from us. And then we should think about trying to get the first dagger. That one's more dangerous, as Dracula has possession of it."

"That's right," said Orlov. "One dagger alone isn't strong enough to give me everlasting beauty."

"Your beauty treatment, Orlov, is not on top of my list of important concerns," said Helsing, shaking his head.

A firm knock sounded at the door.

"Who is it?" asked Helsing, ever suspicious.

"Room service, sir! Come to turn down the beds."

"I'll get it," said Rupert.

"Be careful," warned Helsing. "I sense something isn't right."

Helsing moved to the door. "We can manage, thank you," he said.

There was no reply. "Are you still there?" asked Helsing.

Nothing.

"Open it a fraction," whispered Helsing to Rupert.

Rupert opened the door a crack and saw a bristly, fat-faced man supported by two wooden legs. "*You're* not a member of the hotel staff!" he said.

"No, I'm not," growled Grog. "But I *am* someone

who's come to take a dagger off you." And with that, he bashed Rupert on the head with a mighty fist and burst into the room.

He had no trouble in locating the dagger and sheath. It was displayed on the table before the surprised friends. "*I'll* take that!" he growled, and he reached over and swiped the dagger.

"Oh no you don't," said Rupert, getting to his feet and throwing a fizzing freezing spell at Grog from the burning tips of his fingers.

But Grog ducked in time, and the blue rays of magic light bounced dangerously around the walls of the room.

"I missed," cried Rupert, as Grog darted from the room. "After him!"

Grog was soon trundling clumsily down the corridor on his wooden legs.

"I'll get him!" cried Helsing, racing whippet-like from the room, bounding after Grog and pulling him to the floor, bringing the dagger within his grasp. Or so he thought. No sooner had he brought the thief to the ground, than a bat suddenly appeared and the dagger was snatched away. Helsing looked up to see the precious dagger in the hands – or rather, *claws* – of the bat. Was it tittering away to itself? Helsing thought that it was.

He tried a mighty leap to grab the dagger from the flying bat, but as quickly as it had appeared the bat had vanished. Helsing looked at the floor. So, too, had Grog.

"It's no good," said Helsing, when the others came to help him back on his feet. "Rupert's father took it."

"Father?" frowned Rupert.

Helsing nodded glumly.

"What now?" sighed Klaw.

"Oh dear, oh dear," tutted the professor. "All our efforts have been in vain."

"What about my handsome face?" squeaked Orlov.

"I must chase after Father!" said Rupert, bravely.

"It's worth a try," sighed Helsing. "But, realistically, what are the chances of finding him, let alone getting the dagger back?"

Rupert thought for a moment, then his shoulders slumped. "I suppose the chances are fairly slim," he admitted. "So, what do we do?"

"Return to Transylvania," said Helsing.

"Herr Helsing is quite right," said the professor, perking up. "We know that that is where the dagger is eventually heading. With Krinkelfiend long gone from this particular area, I cannot think of a better plan."

"What a disaster!" hissed Helsing. "We should have moved to a different hotel while we had the chance, then they wouldn't have tracked us down so easily. I've been such a fool!"

"It is too late to worry about what we *should* have done," said the professor, gently, "we must consider what we must do next. And getting on the first available ship would be the right move, in my opinion."

"A ghost?" wondered Orlov with good reason. "The ghost of a monk? Could it be Marvin, the blind monk?"

☙ Chapter Eight
What's Become of Orlov?

Count Krinkelfiend was glad to have departed London. It meant a long time aboard a ship resting inside his coffin, but it was well worth it: worth it now he had returned to Transylvania and was about to break his exciting news to his lord and master, Count Vlad Dracula. Light shimmered on the wall from a dozen tall candles, and the air smelt of warm wax. Yes; this was more like it.

Away from those busy, foggy streets; his errant son, his other enemies, his agents, his. . .

Krinkelfiend's reverie was broken by the sound of creaking floorboards. Dracula's shadow was cast across the entire length of the room. "Oh, master," bowed Krinkelfiend.

"Welcome," said Dracula, in a deep, booming voice. "I trust your venture was a successful one?"

"Oh, most, master, most," said Krinkelfiend, pulling out a leather bag from beneath his cape. "I have the dagger!"

"I know," said Dracula through a thin, bloodless smile. "I can sense its presence."

He held out his long arms, and Krinkelfiend lowered the bag into them. Dracula then turned and moved unhurriedly to a large table. Gently he lifted the second dagger from the bag and laid it on the table.

"Excellent!" he said, stroking the gleaming hilt of the weapon. "What powers I will soon have."

"Shall I fetch the other dagger from upstairs, my master?" asked Krinkelfiend.

"No!" said Dracula, to Krinkelfiend's surprise. "It is too soon."

"Too soon?" he asked, puzzled. "But . . . but we have the two—"

"There is the third dagger yet to come."

Krinkelfiend all but fainted on the spot. "A *third* dagger!" he gasped. "I have read of such things, of course, but I thought that the third dagger was no more than a story, master."

"In a way, it is a story," said Dracula. "But soon it will become reality."

Dracula turned to face the count, when he saw the confusion on his face, he released a long, dismal chuckle.

"Er, what do you wish me to do next, my master?" said Count Krinkelfiend, hoping this wasn't to be the end of his employment.

"You have served me well, Krinkelfiend," said Dracula. "I will continue to use your services for the time being."

Krinkelfiend almost leapt for joy, but managed to control himself. "Oh, master, what honour you bestow on me. What great kindness you—"

"Be quiet, Krinkelfiend."

"As you wish, oh mighty one."

Dracula turned his attention back to the second dagger. "I want more than power," he said, as if he were talking to himself. "I want complete control. One hundred years of darkness will follow when the third dagger is prepared."

"And you can prepare it, master?" asked Krinkelfiend, wondering if this was possible without the daggers' original creator, Marvin. Krinkelfiend knew Marvin was the unique mortal who could control vast energy and contain it inside inanimate objects.

"Of that you will learn more later," said Dracula, putting the dagger back in the bag. "For the next few nights, I shall be busy with the daggers over in Gertcha. I want you there, too. You can keep a close eye on things at the university of Grund, and at Viktoria Palace. I have insiders working for me at the university, and the mortals of Viktoria Palace have no idea of my life beneath their palace." Dracula's eyes glowed in the dimness. "Those are the key places, which will see my powers unfold – as it was planned all those centuries ago."

Krinkelfiend was excited by the prospect; and he'd always had a liking for Viktoria Palace.

"But for the minute," said Dracula, turning to his underling, "let us celebrate your success, Krinkelfiend."

He clicked his fingers and a silver tray holding two goblets of blood appeared on the table.

This was the happiest, if most confusing, night of Krinkelfiend's life.

Helsing and his colleagues, meanwhile, were disembarking their ship, which had taken them from a wharf on the River Thames to the port of Druan, on the Adriatic Sea.

"A long sea journey behind us, at last," said Helsing.

"But a long train journey ahead of us," Rupert reminded them. He glanced towards Professor von Morcumstein. "You seem very quiet, Professor. Is everything all right?"

"What's that? Me? Oh, yes, fine, thank you," said the distracted professor. "I've just been thinking about the two daggers, that is all."

"The two daggers that will give this Dracula chap all the power he wants," said Klaw, joining them on the quay with his case.

"Well, that's just it," said the professor. "Will it give him all the power he wants?"

"So we've been led to believe," said Rupert.

"It had better," said Orlov, "because if they prove useless, then I'll stay ugly!"

"During the sea voyage," said the professor, "I began trying to recall some of my old notes on the daggers and their creator, Marvin the blind monk."

"And?" pressed Helsing.

" 'The day soon approaches when two become three,' " the professor quoted from memory, " 'and one hundred years of darkness and disorder will engulf the earth.' "

"Eh?" said Orlov.

"A quotation, obviously," said Helsing. "One of Marvin's, no doubt. But does it mean that a *third* dagger really exists, Professor?"

"Oh, wonderful," said Orlov, slumping on to his case. "Now it takes *three* daggers to make me beautiful. I could have stayed at home and waited."

"I should have remembered my notes sooner," admitted the professor. "I don't believe Dracula has ended his quest just yet."

"Which is a good thing," said Rupert. "That gives us time to beat him to the third dagger."

"But remember," said the professor, "that Marvin

died from some illness or accident. It is possible that the third dagger was left incomplete."

"So where do you think we should continue our investigation?" asked Klaw. "Transylvania?"

"Grund!" replied the professor, without a moment's hesitation. "The university was a monastery, if you recall. It is where Marvin's first encounter with Dracula took place. Possibly, it is the location where the daggers themselves were created."

"That was four hundred years ago," said Orlov. "We won't find anything at the university in these modern times. I think you'll find the trail's gone a little bit cold."

"If it helps prevent one hundred years of darkness," said Rupert, "then I, for one, think we should listen to the professor."

"One hundred years of ugliness, more like," mumbled Orlov. "I can see it all now. Poor Orlov being buried when his days are over, his ugly, deformed body being lowered into the worm-ridden soil. . ."

As Orlov rumbled on, Klaw smiled. He was very happy about the change in plan. He was heading home.

"So, we are decided on Grund University as our next

port of call?" checked the professor. No one disagreed, though Klaw pointed out that it was his duty to first report to his chief at the police station. "I will join you at the university later," he told them.

It was dusk and drizzling with rain when Inspector Klaw reported back to his office in Grund. He spent the next hour clearing his desk of paperwork, then took a landau up the hillside road to Grund university. There, he joined his colleagues, who were in deep discussion in the principal's office. They had wasted no time in getting to the university after arriving in Grund and establishing themselves in their lodgings.

"Ah, our friend the inspector," said Professor von Morcumstein, looking up.

Helsing and Rupert waved in his direction. Orlov, they had decided, should wait outside.

"Please, do come in," invited Principal Blak, indicating a free chair.

Though an ageing figure, Blak still had a twinkle in his eyes and a firm handshake – as Klaw soon discovered. The most extraordinary feature about him was his hair: he had none, except for one long golden strand, which sprung from his head like a bootlace.

"Your colleagues have been telling me of their interest in reading some of the ancient writings we keep in our vast library," Blak remarked. "Apparently, it is a police matter; confirmed, of course, by your personal appearance, Inspector."

"We are interested in any writings that date back to the time when the university of Grund was the monastery of Grund," explained Klaw. "Particularly those written by the blind monk, Marvin. And I do thank you for your cooperation," he added, politely.

"Quite so," said Blak, almost glumly. "Not much left from those long ago, dark days, of course, but. . ." He shook a bell on his desk. A man appeared from a doorway to an adjacent room. "Ah, Darkak! Could you please provide the inspector and his companions with volumes of work related to ancient writings about the Grund monastery?"

"Er, certainly, Principal," nodded Darkak. "At once!" And he flew from the room almost before he'd entered it.

"I'm sure my secretary won't be long," said Blak, through a thin smile.

Orlov had grown bored waiting outside the principal's office, and had decided to go off for a night-time stroll around the grounds before Inspector Klaw had turned up.

"What an old dump," he thought, as he wandered under arches and down long passageways that intersected other passageways. "Reminds me of Castle Bran," he sniggered. But his sniggering soon stopped. "Oh dear!" he thought. "I'm lost. . .! Yes, there's no doubt about it – Orlov, the king of the creepy corridor, has finally got himself lost."

Orlov strolled beneath an archway, uncertain if he had been there earlier. And then he stopped dead in his tracks.

The hooded, monk-like figure he saw floating before him at first confused him, but then frightened him. His confusion was obvious: the monks left Grund years and years ago. And his fear also was obvious, because the monk didn't simply walk along the passage; he walked straight through the stone walls!

"A ghost?" wondered Orlov with good reason. "The ghost of a monk? Could it be Marvin, the blind monk?"

Orlov knew he had to find the principal's office again to tell them all of his discovery. But he never had a chance to leave the place where he was standing.

Orlov didn't see what hit him, but he knew that whatever it was, hurt. Then he knew nothing more except the blackness into which he fell.

Grog smiled a crooked, mean smile. He picked up both Orlov's uneven feet, and dragged him towards a secret tunnel. Keeping an eye out for trouble for Count Krinkelfiend was proving to be a lot of fun!

"Well, Darkak?" said Principal Blak, as his secretary reappeared in the doorway.

"It's most peculiar, Principal," said the secretary, flustered and mopping his brow with a handkerchief, "but the books. . . !"

"What of them, Darkak?" encouraged Blak.

"They've gone!"

Blak kept his composure and moved gradually back in his chair. "*All* of them?"

"Oh no, sir, all the *usual* books are there; it's just the ancient ones to do with the writings of the monk, Marvin, that have disappeared."

"What can I do other than offer you my apologies, gentlemen!" said Blak, holding out his arms and shaking his head at his visitors.

"It's quite all right," smiled Helsing. "In present circumstances, I would have been surprised to have learned they were still there."

"I cannot help but agree with my friend here." The professor nodded sagely. "In a sense, it confirms our concerns regarding the history of your university, Principal Blak."

"Oh, really?" said Blak, but he was clearly bored by their concerns and eager for them to go. "Well, gentlemen. Again, my apologies. I'm sorry we can be of little further use."

"There is *one* thing," said Helsing.

"Yes?" said Blak, unable to prevent himself from sounding suspicious.

"Would you permit us to return in the morning and spend a little time studying the layout of the university?"

Blak beamed – with relief, it seemed to the others – and said, "Of course, of course. If you feel that that is of some help to your . . . investigation."

"It has more to do with the learned professor's fascination for ancient buildings."

"Quite so!" agreed the professor.

"I understand," bowed the principal, not believing them for a second. "I believe that the professor once lectured at our university."

"Oh, that was a few years back," smiled the professor. "A most enjoyable occasion. Perhaps I should have examined the ancient volumes in the library while I'd had the chance," he added with a chuckle.

A shadow seemed to pass fleetingly across Blak's face. "Er, yes; perhaps you should have, Professor."

"Come on, everyone," said Rupert, suddenly standing and heading for the door. "I think we have taken up enough of the principal's time."

Farewells made, they went out into the corridor to find Orlov. "Where can he have got to?" said Rupert. "Orlov's hopeless at times."

"But surprisingly brilliant at other times," said the professor, thinking of the way he handled himself in London at the auction of the second dagger.

"This is a big place," said Klaw. "Best we search for him together, or we *too* could end up lost."

"Oh, Orlov," tutted Krinkelfiend. "What will
our master say when he hears of your treachery?"

ᗩ Chapter Nine
Into the Spider's Web

Orlov awoke. He opened first one eye, then the other. Then he burst into tears. This wasn't unusual for Orlov. Indeed, he always awoke in this manner. It was how he faced the day ahead; knowing he was the most hideous human being on the planet.

"That's better!" said Orlov, as his tears stopped. "Now, what's going on here? Where am I?"

But the silent, dank room could tell him nothing.

A single torch burned brightly on the nearest wall and, for a brief moment, Orlov thought he was back at Castle Bran, and that Dracula would appear and torture him for his betrayal. But so obsessed was he with rediscovering his beauty, that even the thought of Dracula hardly frightened him any more.

Orlov tried to sit up, which is when he discovered he was bound with ropes to a stone slab. "Maybe I *am* at Castle Bran," he said aloud. "The furnishings seem similar!"

"I assure you, you are not," said a voice from a figure lurking in the shadows behind him.

"Who's that?"

"Oh, Orlov," tutted Krinkelfiend. "What *will* our master say when he hears of your treachery?"

"He probably knows already," said Orlov.

"Very true. But now he will be able to get his hands on you, won't he?"

That, also, was very true, and Orlov knew it. "He might not want to get his hands on me," said Orlov.

"I imagine *no* one would want to get their hands on *you*, Orlov," said Krinkelfiend. "They might catch something fatal."

"Is the master here, then?" asked Orlov, a little nervously.

"Calm yourself, my deformed and almost worthless creature," said Krinkelfiend. "As yet, no one is here but me."

Orlov was uncertain whether that was good or bad news, so chose to say nothing.

"Your colleagues, including the bright but highly irritating Professor von Morcumstein, were no doubt with you at the university earlier?" said Krinkelfiend, slowly and calmly.

"That's right!" said Orlov. "Then some idiot coshed me over the head with something hard."

"Ah yes, that would have been Grog," nodded Krinkelfiend.

"And what was the hard object he struck me with?" asked Orlov.

"His fist!"

"Oh!" Orlov thought about that for a moment. "Well, it's a good job he hit me on the head," he said. "Anywhere else, and it might have been dangerous!"

"Quite so, my gruesome child," smiled Krinkelfiend.

"But what do we do with you?" he pondered.

"You could let me go," said Orlov.

"Not what I had in mind," said Krinkelfiend, seriously. "I think, for the moment, we can keep you where you are. You might make excellent bait for your nosey friends."

"Stay here in this cold, damp cellar!" cried Orlov. "That's monstrous. You're wicked, you are!"

"You are most kind," bowed Krinkelfiend, "but I'm afraid your flattery won't alter my mind."

"And bonkers!" added Orlov, but under his breath.

"Rest in peace!" said Krinkelfiend.

"But you haven't told me where I am."

"No, I haven't!" agreed Krinkelfiend, and then he left the room.

Helsing and his companions were searching the grounds of the university. "He must be here *some-where*," sighed Inspector Klaw. "How could he have gone and got himself so lost?"

"Orlov might not yet be beautiful," said Rupert, "but he's not a complete fool. He proved that in London."

"Meaning?" enquired Helsing.

"That he might not be responsible for his own disappearance," explained Rupert.

"I don't trust that Principal Blak," said Klaw.

"Very wise of you not to," said the professor, as he studied the walls of the corridor they now found themselves in. "He didn't seem exactly concerned that two ancient volumes have gone missing from the university's library. *His* library. *His* responsibility."

"He might be in league with Dracula," said Helsing. "We must never underestimate that vampire's abilities. I remember one of the early wars of the fifteenth century. . . Oh, but that's a long story for another day."

"And one I must have from you for my records," said the professor, turning to glance at Helsing. "The information inside your ancient head is quite priceless."

Helsing smiled in response.

"Well, I know what *I'm* doing," said Rupert, decisively. They all turned to look at him. "I'm going for a little bat-flight to Bran Castle. I want to take a look at things out there from an aerial perspective. I want to see what Dracula is up to, exactly. I might even discover more about the third dagger."

"That could be very dangerous," warned Helsing. "Dracula can sense danger, and even if he's not there, he won't have left the castle unguarded."

"I know, my old friend," said Rupert, "and I'll take the greatest of care. With Orlov missing, the ancient books of Marvin the blind monk, missing . . . the second dagger missing. Well, other than putting my head in the lion's den, we are short on fresh ideas, I would say."

"He has a point, gentlemen," nodded the professor.

"So be it," shrugged Helsing. "But let's agree now to meet you at the Inspector's office tomorrow, mid-day. That way, we'll know where we all are and we can hear about your nocturnal adventures."

Rupert smiled. "Tomorrow midday, it is. And if I'm not back, then assume the worst."

"Very well," said Helsing. "And meanwhile, we will pass the night sneaking further around this university in the cover of darkness."

"We *will*?" said Klaw. "We don't have a warrant of any kind, you know. It's a bit irregular."

"So are vampires!" said Helsing. Klaw didn't disagree.

They decided that it would be safer to at least give the appearance that they were leaving the university premises, so soon all of them were climbing aboard the waiting landau that was destined for the centre of Grund. The cabbie cracked his reins, and the carriage began its slow descent down the darkening hillside.

From his office window, Principal Blak watched unsmiling as the carriage blurred with the darkness and was then gone.

"Darkak!" he hissed.

"Yes, Principal?"

"While it is dark, take the tunnel to Count Krinkelfiend's secret chamber, and update him on what has happened tonight." Then he added, almost to himself. "It was wise we had the old books sent to the count before that lot came snooping."

"I imagine Count Krinkelfiend will know what these people are up to already," said Darkak. "The ugly one was a friend of theirs."

"Nevertheless," insisted Blak, "we are being paid a king's ransom to betray our university. We must give the count his money's worth."

"Yes, Principal," said Darkak, who was beginning to have grave doubts about their treachery now that a local inspector had visited the university.

When the landau was a little further down the hill, Helsing said, "Get ready to jump, everyone. Time to return to the university without being seen!" All but Rupert jumped from the open doors.

"I say," gasped the professor. "I'm not as young as you others. Couldn't we have just climbed down in a more civilized fashion?"

"Too risky," explained Helsing. "It's important that the landau is seen making a steady and continuous descent back to Grund."

"Well, yes, I suppose you're right," said the professor, standing so he could brush down his clothes.

"Keep low, Professor," said Klaw, pulling the elderly man to the ground. "They might have spies out watching for us."

"Really?" grinned the professor, who rather liked that idea. "How terribly exciting."

"We will approach from the east side of the hill," decided Helsing, his face bathed in moonlight. "It is quieter that side – fewer buildings. Easier to approach unseen."

"Very well," said the professor.

"I'm not sure it's any better an idea than Rupert's one of visiting Dracula's castle in Bran," said Klaw. "We could all end up in big trouble tonight."

"We must do something for Orlov," reminded Helsing. "His hours might be numbered if he's in Krinkelfiend's or Dracula's hands."

"He's quite right," nodded the professor. "You see, Orlov committed an act of treachery against Dracula. Vampires do not forgive acts of treachery. You only have to recall how Krinkelfiend behaves towards Rupert."

"Orlov certainly left Dracula to join *our* side," said Klaw. "Yes, I can appreciate that Orlov will not be Dracula's favourite person."

"Correct," said Helsing. "So if we don't try to rescue him, it is certain he will be destroyed – if not tonight, then very soon."

Klaw gulped and followed his colleagues back up the rough terrain towards the dark, foreboding silhouette of the university.

The tunnel burst into light, a thousand flaming torches lining their route downwards.

ᴡᶠ Chapter Ten
A Journey Underground

Itch followed his brother Scratch through the sleeping streets of Bran, Transylvania.

"It was easier when Vermyn lived in a forest in Gertcha," grumbled Itch. "All this travelling's not good for my complexion!"

"Don't worry, little brother," whispered Scratch. "All the kronks that'll soon line your pockets will make the effort worthwhile."

"It better had," said Itch. "Last time you said that, we ended up in prison!"

"That was last time," snapped Scratch. "This is now!"

Scratch pointed to the door of a terraced house in a long street of terraced houses. "That's the place," he beamed. "We've found it, little brother."

Hidden in the shadows of a doorway opposite was a figure. As he watched Itch and Scratch make their arrival, he hurriedly began scribbling down notes – notes intended for Inspector Klaw.

"Come in, quick!" hissed Vermyn, checking the street before tugging the brothers inside. His grin was as formidable as it ever was. These were happy days for Vermyn. The second dagger had been found, yet Count Krinkelfiend *still* wished to retain his employment.

"My employer's boss is taking an immediate vacation," Vermyn explained, when they had reached a dimly lit room to the rear of the small house. "I have been instructed to place you as guard to his castle during his brief absence."

"How many bosses are there?" cried Itch.

Scratch nudged his brother in the midriff. "Keep it shut!" he whispered. "The more paymasters, the more pay. Always think of the kronks, little brother."

"Yes, you're right," giggled Itch. "Forgot. Sorry."

"So, it's a castle we're guarding then?" checked Scratch.

"Yes," grinned Vermyn. "Castle Bran. It stands on the hill behind us, just a little to the west."

"You mean this castle is completely unguarded at the moment?" said Scratch, confused by the idea.

"Well, it is sort of a ruined castle," explained Vermyn. "It is home for one person."

"That being the count's boss?" said Scratch.

"Precisely, though we don't use names or titles here, gentlemen, do we?" grinned Vermyn.

"Don't worry," said Itch. "We'll do the job."

"Excellent. And I'll see you have enough food and water delivered to keep you happy."

"Sounds even better," said Itch, perking up.

"Good," grinned Vermyn. "And if you're ready, there is no time like the present. You will certainly find the castle . . . different!"

Helsing helped Professor von Morcumstein up the crest of the hill, where they all flopped down and waited to recover their breath. "I'm possibly too old to be doing this sort of thing," puffed the professor. "But I cannot resist it, you see."

Helsing and Klaw smiled at each other. The indomitable professor had long had their utmost respect.

"Over there," said Helsing, shifting to get a better look. "The east side of the university. And somewhere inside is Orlov."

"That is not certain, of course," said the professor.

"It isn't?" said Klaw.

"He was kidnapped here. That doesn't mean he has *remained* here," said the professor.

"I suppose it doesn't," admitted the inspector. "Did you ever think of becoming a detective?"

"Oh, no, Inspector," chuckled the professor. "I'm *far* too interested in vampires!"

"Let's assume that Orlov grew bored waiting

for us," said Helsing. "He wouldn't have wandered too far, because he knew we could be out at any moment."

"I think it's dangerous to assume *any*thing with Orlov," sighed Inspector Klaw. "However, you do have a point. He must have been taken near Principal Blak's office."

"There are many corridors in that vicinity," recalled the professor. "It would make a sensible starting place."

Corridor and quadrant, corridor and quadrant. It was quite a maze for the intrepid team. But nothing was to be found. Certainly no trace of poor Orlov.

Suddenly footfalls caught their attention. "Quick! Behind this column," hissed Helsing.

The footfalls grew louder, steadied, then passed by them. "Close," said Helsing, allowing his shoulders to sag. "*Too* close."

"A lecturer?" said Klaw.

"Looked like it," said the professor. "Certainly no spectral image haunting the university."

Klaw gave the professor a nervous glance.

"Only pulling your leg, Inspector," said the smiling professor.

"Well, there's little here to indicate that Orlov was kidnapped," said Helsing, examining the walls of the corridor they now found themselves in.

"And yet. . ." said the professor, measuring his footsteps as he walked the corridor.

"What is it?" asked Klaw in a low voice.

"Have you not noticed something peculiar about this corridor compared with the others?" asked the professor.

"They all look much alike to me," said Klaw.

"It's longer," said Helsing, suddenly cottoning on.

"Yes," said the professor. "And why would it be longer?"

"And very worn in this area by me," said Klaw, pointing to some stonework. "Wait a bit. This stone is loose!"

Klaw tried forcing his fingers around the wobbly stone to get a grip that he could use to pull it free. Helsing snapped his fingers. "You're doing it wrong, Inspector!"

"I am?"

"It needs pushing."

And with that, Helsing leaned over Klaw and used his considerable strength to ram the stone home. The whole section of worn stonework retracted speedily with a whirring sound, exposing a dark tunnel beyond.

"Very vampirish!" nodded the professor. "How they always like to have secret tunnels."

"I think in part it answers the question as to where Orlov went," remarked Klaw.

"Yes, and I think we must see where this tunnel takes us," said Helsing, entering the tunnel around the retracted section of the wall.

Once they were all inside the tunnel, the stone door closed itself behind them.

"Trapped!" cursed Klaw.

"Oh dear!" sighed the professor. "And no light to show us the way."

As if in reaction to his comment, the tunnel burst into light, a thousand flaming torches lining their route downwards.

"How convenient," said Helsing, sarcastically. "An ancient tunnel that illuminates itself."

"Dracula, you think?" said Klaw, seriously.

The professor and Helsing shared a confused look. "Of course it's Dracula, Inspector," said Helsing. "You don't think Orlov put the tunnel here!"

"Yes, yes," said the inspector, slightly embarrassed. "I, er, see what you mean."

"If the story of Marvin is a true one," said the professor as they wandered slowly onwards, "and his missing books in the library would suggest that it is, then why was this tunnel made, if not to benefit Marvin and Dracula?"

"A good point," said Helsing, his voice echoing softly of the damp walls. "And *when* was it made? It appears old, but you can never tell with Dracula, such are his powers."

"I would imagine it to be old," said the professor. "A link between the university, where Marvin lived all that time ago, and another place where Marvin could work unnoticed and in total secrecy on the daggers. Perhaps a place where a forge could be kept for soldering iron and so forth. . ." he pondered.

"That's a thought," said Helsing. "I think all the answers will lie at the end of this neverending tunnel!"

*The roots of a bush behind him lashed themselves
to his throat, choking the life from him.*

✦ Chapter Eleven
Dracula's Garden

Having travelled back to Grund in the landau, Rupert had round a discreet place to effect his transformation into a bat, and he headed towards Dracula's castle. He flew above the castle gates and then circled the castle itself; a place not unfamiliar to him. He remembered the cubbyhole in the panelled room where Dracula had secreted the first dagger; the fight in the nearby fields when his father had transformed into a two-headed dragon; his first meeting with Vlad Dracula inside the castle. Yes, it all came back in one mighty gush.

And now, as he flew ever closer to the walls and turrets, he saw that, other than two dozing men at the main gates, it appeared to be deserted. Everything appeared to be taking place around Grund, bearing out the importance of Marvin and the town's university.

"Oh well," sighed Rupert, falling gently to the ground and simultaneously transforming back into human form, "no harm in inspecting Dracula's grounds."

He stole around in the dark for some while, avoiding the moonlight, which illuminated the gardens and could give him away. "So empty and silent," he mused. "This seems wrong. It's as though I'm in a trap, yet I can't understand why or what that trap might be!"

His vampire senses were sharp. Rupert was, indeed, in a trap. Nearby, he heard a rustling from one of the bushes. At once he threw himself to the ground, aware of danger. He kept perfectly still and waited. He didn't have to wait long. One of the bushes to his right was rustling, and for a very good reason: it was crawling along the lawn on its roots towards him.

Rupert raised an arm to cast an immediate spell upon the bush that would stop its progress, but the bush was quicker than he. It threw a long, sinewy root at his arm, wrapping it around his wrist, and rolling him over on his side. Then other roots from the bush reached out and secured his legs, dragging him towards it.

All Rupert could think was how silly it was that he was about to be eaten by a magic bush!

Now other bushes and large plants started to come alive in Dracula's enchanted garden. Rupert struggled to free his feet, managing to free only one of them, with which he began to kick out wildly at the creeping roots.

Just as he thought he was getting the upper hand, the roots of a bush behind him lashed themselves to his throat, choking the life from him. With his free arm, he patted desperately at his jacket pocket, found and pulled out a penknife. Clasping it in his palm, he pressed a catch on the side, and a silvery blade flew open.

Without losing a second, Rupert slashed out at all the roots holding him, which at once retreated with painful squeals. Then he cut away the worst root of all, the one at his throat.

"AARGH!" he cried, gasping for, and finding air at last.

Before they could regroup for another attack, Rupert sprinted across the lawn.

"Safe!" he gasped, which was when Itch and Scratch fell upon him.

"Who are you?" demanded Scratch, holding Rupert's arms behind his back.

"Er. . . I have my identity papers in my pocket, if you'll allow me to show you?" said Rupert, cleverly. He'd have done anything to free his dangerous hands.

"Not so fast," said Itch. "We want answers."

The moonlight caught their faces, and Rupert recognized the two brothers from the auction room in London.

"Answers to what?" said Rupert.

"Well, answers to . . . answers to. . ." said Itch, not really that sure.

"Answers to why you are here?" Scratch said helpfully.

"Yes," agreed Itch. "Why *are* you here? We're guarding this castle, and we're not to let strangers go wandering about the place."

"I see," said Rupert, quickly thinking. "Well, the thing is, gentlemen, I'm the gardener!"

"Eh?" said Itch.

"Gardeners don't work at night," said Scratch.

"Ah, but they do at *this* castle," smiled Rupert. "You must have heard all about the owner, you being the guards of this fine castle?"

"Yes, well. . ." began Scratch. "We know a *little* bit. But that's not the point," he snapped. "We're to ask *you* the questions."

"Yes," nodded Rupert, "and I have told you: I am the gardener. Now, if you let me go, I will show you my papers."

"Sounds reasonable." Itch shrugged.

Scratch reluctantly released Rupert's arms.

Rupert slowly stood. "Thank you, gentlemen. And if you try to move, you will now find that that is not possible."

Itch looked at Scratch who looked at Itch.

"It's that chap from London!" cried Itch, trying un-successfully to move his legs. "What've you done to us?"

"Where's Dracula?" asked Rupert.

"Who?" said Itch, genuinely confused.

"All we know is what Vermyn told us," said Scratch, frantically trying to move his feet, but they wouldn't budge an inch. "He mentioned something about Viktoria Palace in Grund, but he tells us nothing important. Honest. Let us go, now. PLEASE!"

"Very well," said Rupert. "Give it five minutes, gentlemen, and you will find you will be back to normal. Then you can return to the gates where you're supposed to be."

With that, Rupert burst into bat-form, climbing higher and higher into the night sky. He didn't stop or look back until he had returned to Grund.

"This tunnel appears to have no end," remarked Inspector Klaw to his companions, Professor von Morcumstein and Helsing. "We must have walked over two miles!"

"Wherever it leads," said Helsing, "it is clearly a long way from the university. But if Dracula created it, and Orlov was taken down it, then we know it must lead *some*where."

"I must say, all this exercise is giving me quite an appetite," remarked the professor. "It's been quite some time since we last ate anything."

And then, just as the professor had finished speaking, the tunnel ended. Quite literally. A blank stone wall blocked their path.

"This appears to be the end of our journey," said Helsing.

"*Now* what?" asked Klaw, casting an eye around the tunnel. "There don't appear to be any loose stones here to release a secret door. This is certainly the absolute end of the road."

"Above us," said the professor, quietly.

"Well spotted," smiled Helsing. "It's a trap door of some kind, but it's too high to reach."

Klaw bent over. "Not if you climb on my back, it isn't!" he said.

Helsing jumped on to the inspector's bent back, and managed to thread a hand through the metal ring of the door's handle. "Here goes!"

He pulled sharply in a downwards motion.

The door at first creaked angrily back, but then, in one sudden gush, gave way completely.

"Whoops!" cried Helsing, as he rolled off Klaw's back and bounced on the solid ground.

"My dear Helsing," said the professor, rushing over to him. "Have you broken anything?"

"Broken anything?" chuckled Helsing. "I didn't even bruise myself."

"You didn't even. . ." Then the professor remembered. "Ah, yes. You Immortal Ones are made of stronger stuff. How silly of me to forget."

"Come, gentlemen," called Klaw, staring up into the room above them. "Let's help each other through this trap door."

"It's a kind of cellar," whispered Klaw, after they had struggled with some difficulty into the space above.

"An overhead cellar!" remarked the professor. "Well, *that's* unusual."

"Very gloomy here," said Helsing.

"There's a little light coming from around that wall," said Klaw, pointing.

And as they walked around the wall, they were instantly aware that someone else was in the room.

"MMPHFH!"

"Who are you?" asked Klaw nervously, not seeing much as his eyes hadn't yet become accustomed to the dimness.

"MMPHFH!"

"I have a feeling it is Orlov," said the professor, striding across to the prostrate figure of their deformed friend. "A gagged and bound Orlov," he smiled. "How are you, Orlov?"

Helsing tore out the handkerchief that had been wedged in Orlov's mouth. "Oh, really fine, thanks! I love being tied to a stone slab in a room that I've never been in before by a crazy vampire. It's my idea of a great night out!"

"Yes, we can understand you are a little upset—" began the professor.

"UPSET!" cried Orlov.

"Quiet," said Helsing. "We might be heard."

They quickly untied Orlov, who then got groggily to his feet and looked at them with a suspicious frown. "How did you manage to get by Krinkelfiend and his heavy, Grog?"

"We never came across them," shrugged Helsing.

"Which means," he went on, suddenly cautious, "they must be somewhere above us, wherever *above* is, exactly. Do you know where *above* is, Orlov?"

Orlov shook his crooked head. "Krinkelfiend wouldn't tell me."

"Then I think we must make the discovery for ourselves," said Helsing.

Rupert landed in a quadrangle of Grund University, just as the bell in the tower chimed five times. "Another hour," he thought, "and the university will surely be awake."

He was hoping to find his friends still searching for Orlov, but was disappointed to find that wasn't the case. So, instead, he decided it might be worth visiting the library. "It would be interesting to see if Marvin's written works have made a miraculous return to the university shelves."

His journey was an easy one. There was literally no one around at that hour. He turned the handle on the library door. "Locked!" he thought, but was untroubled by the inconvenience. He merely pointed a finger at the handle and the keyhole, and it unlocked itself for him and the door gently opened.

"Thank you," whispered Rupert, entering the room.

The library was vast. Shelf upon shelf of ancient and modern books adorned the walls from floor to ceiling. "Most impressive!" he thought.

His gaze moved across the silent rows of books. The portraits on the walls of former college principals – long-dead principals – stared blankly down upon him. "Good job I'm half vampire," he thought, "or this place would give me the creeps!"

Checking the titles on the appropriate shelf, he soon discovered that the books by Marvin – and all other books referring to the blind monk, it seemed – were missing. "Did Blak arrange their removal?" he wondered.

Then Rupert froze. He could hear the *click, click* footfalls of someone beyond the library door.

"What type of shoe could make such a sound?" he asked himself. His answer soon came.

Into the room lunged a lantern, followed by a bearded, sneering face and pear-shaped body: a body supported by two strong wooden legs!

"WHO'S HIDING IN HERE?" shouted Grog,

clip-clopping further into the library. "Come on, now. Don't think you can get away from *me*!"

Rupert deliberately didn't act straight away. The wooden-legged man was clearly very confident, and Rupert could recall the last time they had met. It was quite possible that Dracula was protecting him.

Instead, Rupert remained crouched by the book shelf and waited. Grog soon spotted him, and strode noisily forward, his vast, muscle-bound arms poised angrily above his head.

"ARGHH! BIG GROG'S GOING TO SQUASH YOU LIKE A FLY!" he threatened, moving ever closer to the silent and still Rupert.

When just a couple of feet away from him, Rupert rolled back, pulling the rug he had been kneeling upon with him.

"WHAT THE. . . ?" cried Grog, as his hefty frame flew backwards and, with a sickening thud, struck the wooden floor beneath. All was silent.

"Sleep well!" said Rupert, clambering to his feet. He grabbed the lantern from the fallen Grog, and sneaked out of the room.

Rupert wasn't sure what his next move should

be, except that the adventure had begun some years ago in Viktoria Palace, and that Itch and Scratch had mentioned the same palace.

Rupert sat down upon a low wall at the edge of the quadrangle in which he had landed. "Could it be possible that there was – still is – a link between the two oldest buildings in the vicinity; Grund university and Viktoria Palace?" he pondered. "If *I* was working on magical daggers at the university, I wouldn't want to risk being seen. I suppose I *would* go looking for another hiding place. And there wasn't much around here except the palace in those long-ago days – at least few places large enough to hide such activities." Rupert shrugged.

The bell chimed six times. The signal for the beginning of another day of life at the university. "I'll hang around the town for a while, then meet up with the others in the inspector's office," Rupert decided, and with that he took to the air.

A few minutes later, he was above the town centre. He found a quiet spot to land and transformed back to his true human appearance.

"Who are you, and what are you doing in the king's home?" came a voice…

⚐ Chapter Twelve
A Breakfast with Surprises

"So, what's the plan?" said Orlov, glad to be free of his stone bed.

Professor von Morcumstein checked his watch that hung on a chain from his waistcoat. "It is six in the morning," he said. "Daylight will be with us. It is safe to explore the surrounds without the risk of a vampire crossing our path."

"Grog isn't a vampire," said Orlov, rubbing his

head, which still felt sore from where Dracula's beefy employee had struck him.

"We can worry about Grog if and when we bump into him," Helsing assured him. "Now come, friend Orlov. Let's explore!"

The first thing they came across was a ladder leading to another trap door. "A ladder upwards," said Klaw. "It seems we really *are* in a cellar above the tunnel."

Orlov shook the ladder a few times.

"What do you make of it, Orlov?" asked Helsing.

"It's a ladder!" said Orlov, stupidly.

"We all assumed as much," said Helsing. "Let's climb up it and see what we see."

Helsing was first up. "It seems a very grand place," said Helsing, calling back down to the others. "I'm standing in a small alcove next to a grand hallway with large rooms running off it."

The professor was next to stick his head out. "I know this place," he said.

"So do I," said Klaw, joining him.

"I don't!" said Orlov.

"This is Viktoria Palace," explained the professor.

"Home to King Konstantine and his daughter Princess Lashka."

"*And* home to the first dagger," added Klaw.

"Interesting," said Helsing. "A link of sorts between the university and the palace. They must be the oldest buildings in Grund."

"Certainly around at the time Dracula first trod the earth," agreed the professor.

"Who are you, and what are you doing in the king's home?" came a voice from near them.

They turned to see Walter, the king's head butler. Walter at once recognized the professor and Inspector Klaw. "Oh, gentlemen," he gasped. "Er, what a surprise. What brings you here?"

"A tunnel!" said Orlov.

"It's a long story," said Klaw, "but it involves vampires and your old friend Count Krinkelfiend."

Walter shuddered. "I thought all that had been dealt with years ago," he said.

"In a way, it was," said the professor. "But these vampires are not so easily removed as mere mortals."

"I'm sorry to hear that," said Walter, meaningfully. After a short, contemplative pause, he asked them if they would like something to eat. "The king won't be up for a little while, so I can prepare the breakfast room for you. You must be very hungry after your tour beneath the palace." He noticed Orlov for the first time and took a hasty step back.

"Don't mind me," said Orlov. "I used to be handsome!"

"Er, yes, I see," croaked Walter. "Come with me, gentlemen."

"I hadn't expected to emerge from the darkness to a cooked breakfast," smiled the professor to Helsing. "What a pleasant surprise."

Not long after they'd first arrived at the palace Helsing, Orlov, Inspector Klaw and Professor von Morcumstein were enjoying a hearty breakfast.

"Thank you for your hospitality, Walter," said the professor. "Orlov, please pass me the salt."

"What does it look like?" said Orlov, searching the table with his crooked eyes. Klaw passed the professor the salt.

"We need to base ourselves here for the night," Helsing told Walter. "Below your cellar there is, as you will have heard us mention earlier, a secret tunnel. It links to the university, and we believe it is used as a route by the vampires. Indeed, we are certain that Vlad Dracula, lord of all vampires, created this tunnel himself some centuries ago. Perhaps he then shut it down, but whatever, he has now chosen to reopen it. To deal with him and prevent his dreadful plans from succeeding, we need to be here."

"That is quite all right, sir," bowed Walter. "The staff will be alerted, and put at your disposal. You need only to make a request, and, however trivial, it will be carried out."

"That is most accommodating of you, Walter," Helsing thanked him.

"Are you still hungry, at all?" asked Walter.

"Yes," said Orlov. "I'm so hungry, I could eat a horse! In fact, I did once. That was back in 1499, when—"

"Enough, Orlov," sighed Helsing.

"Oh, right!"

Then, with a large, hideous grin, Orlov forced an entire bread roll into his mouth without breaking it first.

"Hurry up, Orlov," said Helsing. "We need to get to the inspector's office and meet up with Rupert to share our news."

After Helsing and his companions had left for the police station, Walter went to the king's room. He knocked and knocked, but there came no answer. "How strange!" he thought. He opened the door a fraction. "Your Majesty?" he called.

Walter peered around the edge of the door and gasped. There, standing before him, was the bearded figure of the king. But it was a stone figure – the same sort of stone figure that Walter himself had once been transformed into. "Oh no," he cried. "The nightmare is returning to the palace again."

He went to the princess's room and it was the same sad story. The princess and her lady in waiting were both frozen stone figures, the lady caught in the act of brushing her mistress's hair.

Rupert was already in the inspector's office when they returned from the palace. Between them, they updated each other on the previous night's adventure. "Funny," said Rupert, "but I sensed there was some link between the palace and the university. All my vampire senses began to tell me so. But a *tunnel*!" He shook his head in surprise.

"So, what is the plan for tonight?" asked Inspector Klaw.

"I think we need to hide in the tunnel – or at least, the palace cellar," said Helsing. "Things are bound to happen, then we can just see what we see. It's not easy to have a clever plan mapped out when you are dealing with vampires."

"Very true," nodded Rupert.

"Krinkelfiend *and* Dracula," said the Professor. "Now that *is* going to be interesting."

"Yes, tonight should reveal much," said Helsing.

"Let's hope we survive it," said Rupert.

Klaw shuddered at his words.

A little later, and despite their fatigue, the friends returned to Viktoria Palace, leaving Klaw to spend the rest of the day in his office to catch up on work. He made a report for the chief – one he hated doing as he had to talk of vampires and mysterious daggers, which never went down well with the chief – then rifled through all the messages and telegrams on his desk.

"Ah-*ha*!" he said, when finding one in particular; one he had hoped would be waiting for him.

131

He grinned as he read. It was from Officer Brokjaw, a man he'd sent to Bran with the specific task of looking out for three known criminals – Vermyn and the Ripaka Brothers, aka Itch and Scratch.

Brokjaw's message read as follows: "Have located threesome from doorway in street on night of 12th. The two brothers entered house at eight in the evening. Main suspect, V—, seen talking to them, then all three went inside."

"Excellent!" said Klaw, carefully filing the paper. He then picked up the phone on his desk and dialled a number. "I need a team to set off immediately for Bran, Chief." A pause. "Yes, Bran in Transylvania." A pause. "Not our area, I know, sir. Thing is, it is vital to that case I'm on. The one you don't like me talking about." A further pause. "Thank you, Chief."

Klaw replaced the receiver with a flourish and sat down back in his chair.

"KRAKNUT!" he called out, almost making himself jump.

"Yes, Inspector?" said Kraknut from the office across the hall.

"I want you to take three strong men up to Grund university tonight."

"Right, Inspector," Kraknut called back. "Er, any particular reason, sir?"

"Yes, I have a couple of tasks for you there involving a potentially crooked principal and his secretary, and a secret tunnel that needs watching. And you can come in here now and learn all about it."

"Oh, right sir," said Kraknut, scraping back his chair.

Walter, the king's head servant, rushed to greet the arriving men. "Oh, gentlemen," he gasped. "Something *awful* has happened."

"Hello, Walter," said Rupert. "How have you been keeping?"

"Oh, well, sir, well . . . until now, that is."

"What's the matter?"

"The king and Princess Lashka," cried Walter. "They've been turned to . . . to stone!"

"Father, I bet," sighed Rupert. "Just his sort of thing."

Rupert went alone to the king's private quarters. Once inside and confronted by the statue of

King Konstantine, Rupert extended his fingers, which sizzled as he spoke the words:

"By the forces of blue,
Let flesh be renewed."

With a huge explosion that sent Rupert backwards and slammed him against the nearest wall, ten blue flames fizzed out of his fingers and smashed into the statue that was the king. But the result was not quite what Rupert had had in mind. The flames deflected from the statue and shot all over the room like a box of fireworks accidentally let off. Rupert ducked as a flame brushed across some of his hair, turning it into grey dust.

"A bit dangerous, that," he muttered, brushing the stone dust off his head. "No better than the spell I used on that wooden-legged chap in London." He thought for a moment. "It could be one of Father's spells, all right. It is *very* strong. I should be able to free it, unless . . . unless it is *Dracula* who turned the king and princess to stone. *No* one could break one of *his* spells."

Rupert looked at the end of his fingers, which still smoked softly. Then he looked back at the poor king. "One more go!" he decided.

The blue flames flashed against the statue, and. . .

"Ah, there you are, my boy," said the professor, peering into the room – just at the wrong moment.

"Oh dear!" said Rupert, tapping the newly formed statue of Professor von Morcumstein. "It's only a *deflected* spell," explained Rupert, to the solid professor. "It'll only last a minute or two. Only direct hits are permanent."

In fact, as he spoke, the stone dissolved into dust revealing the true, if somewhat dusty, professor.

"My, my," said the professor. "I was, er, just wondering what you were up to. I appear to have found out!"

Rupert frowned at the statue of the king. "Sadly, I'm not up to very much," he sighed. "I can't break through the original spell. I'm afraid the king and his daughter will have to remain on display like this for the time being."

"Then come downstairs," urged the professor.

135

"Helsing has made a very interesting find, which I'm sure will fascinate you."

In the palace library, Helsing was poring over the two volumes of Marvin the blind monk's writings. Orlov was strewn across a sofa, half-asleep. This was very off-putting, as half-asleep to Orlov meant sleeping with only one eye closed.

"Ahh," said Helsing, as the professor and Rupert entered the study. "Both volumes," he said, pointing at the large, decaying books. "I discovered them in the library, hidden among a multitude of other books."

"Disguised in the manner that the daggers were originally disguised – with many others so that they would be less easily detected," recalled the professor, moving towards the volumes. "Marvin's writings," the professor whispered to Rupert.

"No wonder they weren't in the university library when I looked," said Rupert.

The professor reached across Helsing and delicately turned a page. "The books are so old they have mostly faded and crumbled away."

"Yes, they're mostly illegible," said Helsing,

moving out of the way to allow the learned professor the opportunity for a closer inspection.

"But they appear quite genuine," nodded the professor. He moved to the second volume, deliberately opening it near the end of Marvin's writings. "Now this is interesting," he said, after a long while. He pulled a magnifying lens from his coat pocket. "Yes. Listen to this, please." And the professor began to read a passage aloud. " 'And after the Dark One came and took control of my unique powers. . .' It fades for a bit, after that," said the professor. "Ah, here we are. It continues, '. . .thus in one month the first dagger was prepared by furnace in secrecy in a tunnel beneath the foundations of Viktoria Palace. The jewels were set – such wonderful jewels, large enough to contain all the energy I could drain from the air and force into them. The flawless Burmese ruby is the master jewel, containing, in such a small space, all the force of a hundred volcanoes. The Dark One, who threatens one hundred years of darkness, commands me to prepare another for his use. The two daggers combined would make him invincible. I am unable to refuse his commands, as he controls a part of my mind at his whim. I fear he wishes me to prepare a third dagger after the completion of the second. That would be dangerous, and I have told him so. But still he hints that he is not happy that there should be but two mighty weapons in his cold hands. . .' The writing fades again," explained the professor. He carefully turned the page. "Here we are. 'The Dark One gives me no rest. The second dagger is complete, the third is in preparation. My health, both in body and mind, is weakening with each exhausting day. I know not how much more I can take of this. . .' "

All eyes were on the professor. "Well?" said Helsing. "Do you think he died soon after writing those words?"

"Or did he finish the third dagger?" the professor continued. "*That* is the big question, I would say, gentlemen."

"Worked to death by Dracula," mused Rupert.

"I know the feeling," said Orlov, stretching and yawning on the sofa.

"The third dagger must, in part, exist," said the

professor, "or Dracula would have acted on the two now in his possession."

"Could he have finished it himself, Professor?" asked Rupert.

"That would depend how near completion it had been," replied the professor. "Marvin gives little clue as to how far he had progressed with his work on the third dagger. Personally, I believe it was this blind monk, Marvin, and his strangely unique talent for trapping the energies around us and concentrating them into these daggers, that was the crucial element. Dracula is powerful, but Marvin was special. But Marvin died so long ago. Could an incomplete dagger still be of any danger to man?"

"Well, I saw a monk before that wooden-legged idiot bashed me on the head," said Orlov.

Slowly everyone turned to look at Orlov. Orlov felt uncomfortable. "Honest, I did! He walked through a wall in the corridor near that principal chap's office."

"Marvin, alive?" gasped the professor. "*That* would explain things very clearly."

Suddenly Marvin the blind monk grabbed one of the two remaining weapons and thrust it deep into Dracula's chest.

Chapter Thirteen

The Daggers Unite

"**W**atching over an empty castle has to rate as one of the most boring jobs in the world," said Itch.

"Maybe we should have gone back into Bran and told old grinning face about our visitor," said Scratch.

"Not after watching him turn into a bat," shivered Itch. "He'd never have believed us."

It was midday, and he was sitting with his

brother Scratch outside the main gates of Castle Bran, lazily chucking stones at some object on the ground.

"But you're right, little brother," agreed Scratch. "It *is* boring here. I mean, who's going to come along in broad daylight to visit an old ruin like this?"

"Exactly!" said Itch. "So, tell me this."

"Yes?"

"Why are those uniformed policemen running up the hillside towards us, waving truncheons?"

Scratch stared ahead. "RUN FOR IT!"

Meanwhile, Vermyn was counting out money at his secret address in Bran village. His personal share amounted to many kronks. Not enough to retire, but enough to keep him out of trouble for a long while.

There came a knocking at his door. "What do those idiot brothers want *this* time?" he muttered, moving to the door. "I told them to keep guard at the castle." Then he called out, "Coming, coming," and opened the door a little.

The door was pushed back into his face, and two sturdy police officers jumped inside. "Vermyn Vladik Rubberkik?"

"Er . . . perhaps."

"You are under arrest for aiding and abetting a felony."

In the street beyond the officers, sat a morose-looking Itch and Scratch in a caged carriage.

Vermyn's grin turned sour on his lips. His hands were cuffed, and he was tossed into the back of the carriage with his partners in crime.

"All the kronks in the world, my foot," moaned Itch. "Wealth beyond all our dreams. What nonsense!"

"It's *his* fault," said Scratch, rattling his chains at Vermyn, who was crouched opposite them.

"So, it's back to prison then, gentlemen," said Vermyn, surprisingly still grinning.

"And if we ever escape, I'll be first to wring your neck!" promised Scratch.

"Me, too!" said Itch.

"You can't," said Scratch. "*I'm* first."

"We can *both* be first," said Itch.

"How?"

"Well, we'll do it at the same time."

Vermyn began shaking his head, and then he

burst into loud sobs. Itch and Scratch, who had seen many odd things in their troubled lives, found watching a grinning man cry one of the oddest!

In a secret chamber that ran off the tunnel stretching from Grund University to Viktoria Palace, and which was very close to the opening beneath the cellar of Viktoria Palace, sat Vlad Dracula. The chamber held many happy memories for him; memories of the early years when a giant furnace had raged while Marvin worked his magic over the glowing daggers. And now it had raged again in this very room, all these years later. "Revenge on these mortals who hate vampires will soon be mine," thought Dracula, sitting tall in his throne-like chair. Before him, looking less relaxed, stood Krinkelfiend.

"Tonight marks the coming together of the three daggers," Dracula explained in a cold, toneless voice.

"And then your powers will be unlimited, my lord."

"Precisely," said Dracula. "'One hundred years of

darkness will follow', as it is so written." Then Dracula leant forward. "And I don't want Helsing interfering. He is not mortal, and therefore he is dangerous to me. My powers against him are limited and unreliable. I know this from past experience."

"He shall be dealt with, my master," bowed Krinkelfiend.

"Just make sure he is out of the way until my work is finished. And tonight, it *will* be finished."

"Most exciting, my lord," fawned Krinkelfiend, while wondering where he might fit in with the vampire's long-term plans.

"After tonight, you may continue to serve me permanently if you so choose," said Dracula, sensing Krinkelfiend's aspirations.

"Oh, my lord and master," cried Krinkelfiend, overcome by the honour. He fell to his knees and began kissing Dracula's feet.

"I've told you before about drooling over my shoes," Dracula reminded him.

"Oh yes," said Krinkelfiend, quickly standing up. "I forgot."

"I want no intrusions tonight," warned Dracula.

"Make sure that *all* Helsing's associates, including Orlov, are contained."

"It shall be done, oh great one," said Krinkelfiend. "As for my former son, Rupert. . ."

"What of him?"

"He is part vampire. Perhaps you will allow me to turn him into a pet? I have always fancied a three-headed dog."

"Then so be it," said Dracula. "Destroying another vampire – even one who has crossed to the path of good – is impossible, and any attempt un-acceptable by vampire law: Law that I, Vlad Dracul, created. Treat him well, Krinkelfiend, but never allow him to return to his normal form."

"I'll feed him twice a night and walk him before sunrise every morning," Krinkelfiend promised solemnly.

Professor von Morcumstein, Orlov, Helsing and Rupert spent the afternoon absorbed by the two volumes of Marvin's writings.

"Other than the question of whether the dagger was completed or not," said the professor, "the most intriguing thing is Orlov's claim to have seen a monk."

"I really did," said Orlov, who had now left the sofa and joined the others around the books. "He disappeared through the wall of the corridor near the principal's office."

"Well, we know all about that corridor and its false wall with a secret door," said Helsing.

"But would it be possible for Dracula to recreate Marvin from . . . from his remains?" winced Rupert, thinking the notion rather repulsive.

"*Any*thing is possible with Dracula," said Helsing, meaningfully. Then he added, matter-of-factly. "Of course, I met Marvin."

"You . . . *met* him?" gasped the professor.

Helsing's eyes glazed over. "All that time ago," he sighed, wistfully. "We met just the once, while I was trying to spy on Dracula. I knew something was happening at the monastery – university, I suppose I should call it now. Marvin was too frightened to tell me anything. I'm not sure he trusted me. Perhaps he thought it was a trap, and that I was working for Dracula. By the time he realized he could have trusted me, it was too late."

"When I first visited Grund University some years ago, just before all this adventure with the daggers began," said the professor, "I was told that his spirit was often seen floating around the college at night. Maybe it wasn't just Marvin's spirit, but his whole recreated body. Maybe even then, Dracula, though not visible to man at the time, was controlling Marvin – preparing him for the task ahead."

"What a horrible thought!" said Rupert. "Poor Marvin. Even in death, Dracula gives him no peace."

"Tonight we must observe closely," said Helsing, "and if the chance arrives to steal a dagger or two, then we must do so. Or, rather, Rupert must do so. There is no guarantee that now Dracula has possession of them the daggers will let anyone else hold them except another vampire."

"I'll give it a go," shrugged Rupert. "I've nothing to lose."

As evening approached, and the sun began to set in the west, Inspector Klaw joined the team at Viktoria Palace.

"I think the time is upon us, gentlemen," said Helsing. "We must move to the cellar where Orlov is supposed to be tied up, and await the return of Krinkelfiend."

"*And* the daggers," added Orlov. "No daggers, no beautiful me!"

"We should tell Walter and thank him for his hospitality," said the professor.

"Quite right," agreed Helsing. "Er . . . where is Walter, by the way?"

"Come to think of it, where are *any* of the staff?" said Rupert.

"Let's take a quick look around," suggested Inspector Klaw.

The professor looked through a window. "We mustn't linger for too long," he warned. "It's dark now. The vampires will be rising at any time."

They started on the ground floor, soon coming to the giant ballroom, so familiar to the Professor, Rupert and Klaw from their first visit to the palace some years ago.

"Look!" gasped Rupert.

"Oh no!" said Helsing.

All the staff, including Walter, were stone statues, just like the king and the princess in their rooms upstairs.

"How has Father managed to turn everyone into stone again, and not even be inside the building?"

"Who said I *wasn't* in the building?" came a voice.

"Where did *that* come from?" said Orlov, his eyes searching the room, but in different directions.

Count Krinkelfiend swooped down from the chandelier that hung from the centre of the ceiling, bursting from bat into man as he did so.

Straightening his top hat, he moved closer to the group. "Helsing, too," he sneered. "You might be an Immortal One," he said, "but you can't stop me now. I'm shielded by Dracula himself."

"No wonder I couldn't break his statue spell earlier," thought Rupert.

"What do you want, Krinkelfiend?" said Helsing, very calm because he knew that the vampire had always been afraid of him. Helsing's Immortal status made it impossible for any of Krinkelfiend's spells to be truly effective.

"I believe he intends preventing us from

interfering with Dracula's plans for the three daggers," said the professor, studiously.

"Ah, Professor von Morcumstein," bowed Krinkelfiend. "As usual, you are quite correct in your summing up of the situation. It is an honour – indeed, a privilege – to have the opportunity, once again, of destroying you."

"How kind," acknowledged the professor, genuinely touched by the vampire's words.

"And I see my somewhat silent former son is among us this evening."

"Father, you really must start behaving yourself before something awful happens," said Rupert. "Dracula cannot be certain that it is safe to combine the power of the three daggers. . ."

"SILENCE!" growled Krinkelfiend. He glanced over his shoulder. "And where do you think you are going, Orlov? You might have escaped once, but it will not happen again!"

"Er, back to the slab, is it then?" grinned Orlov, hideously.

"Droll but true, oh ugly one," said Krinkelfiend. "You are, in fact, *all* going on the slab. Now move towards the cellar, please. You too, Helsing, unless you want me to obliterate your friends on the spot."

Rupert flew a hand out at his father, sending a blinding ray of red light shooting towards the vampire's head. But it struck him and bounced away, fizzing out completely after a few moments. Krinkelfiend just laughed.

"I've not been having much luck at this lately," sighed Rupert under his breath.

"Forcefield spells never last," Helsing told Krinkelfiend.

"Perhaps not, but they last long enough to see you lot safely dealt with, I assure you."

At that same moment, at Grund University, Principal Blak and his secretary were loading cash into two suitcases. Money that Dracula had paid them for their deceit.

"Hurry!" urged Blak. "The sooner we're away from this place the better."

"Yes, Principal," said Darkak, nervously.

"Going somewhere, gentlemen?" said Sergeant Kraknut, appearing in the office doorway.

Without faltering, Blak shouted "RUN!" as he himself darted for the door. The secretary remained rooted to the spot; defeated and disappointed.

Kraknut grabbed Blak by the legs and brought him tumbling to the floor. "It's the handcuffs for you, my man!" he said. But before he could attach them, Blak had bitten his arm and made it to the doorway.

"STOP HIM!" called Kraknut, rubbing his sore arm. One of the officers at once did. With his fist!

Blak saw stars twinkling around his head, then he smiled in a vague, distant way before falling to the ground – again!

"Are you going to try and make a run for it, too?" asked Kraknut turning on the secretary.

"Oh, er, no, sir," squeaked Darkak, holding up his wrists to be cuffed.

"I have prepared a rather large slab for you, as you can see," the count told his prisoners, who were secured by ropes to the stone slab, head to toe in a line.

"You won't get away with this," said Klaw, unconvincingly.

"Why ever not?" asked Krinkelfiend.

Klaw couldn't think of an answer, so remained quiet.

Krinkelfiend smiled. "How appropriate that our local inspector should be confident to the last. Perhaps when our work is done tonight, I will have you shrunk and placed on my mantelpiece in Castle Windfall. You would make a perfect memento of this wonderful time."

Krinkelfiend waved a gentle arm at the cellar. "Do make yourself at home, gentlemen. I shall return shortly with someone most anxious to see that some harm has come to you. And don't try any magic in this room, my former son," he warned. "My lord and master has created a reverse spell on anything attempted in these quarters. You will only end up damaging yourself."

Krinkelfiend made to leave the room, but abruptly stopped. "Just a minute . . . where's Helsing?" he said.

That was a good question. He clearly wasn't on the slab, and no one had seen him disappear. Krinkelfiend paused and then laughed dismissively.

"The fool! There is nowhere he can hide from me," warned Krinkelfiend. "If he attempts to free you, he will not succeed. This cellar is under the influence of my lord and master. So warn him to try nothing. Meanwhile," and here he smiled, a cruel and unpleasant smile, "make yourselves comfortable in my absence."

Krinkelfiend disappeared behind the wall, which led to the hidden trap door and into the tunnel.

"Where can he have got to?" whispered Klaw, when they were left alone.

"He is an Immortal One," explained Professor von Morcumstein. "Helsing has been waiting to trap Vlad Dracula. You can be sure he has a plan of which we know nothing. After all," he added, "he's been waiting centuries for this moment, just as Dracula has been waiting centuries to unify the daggers."

"Meanwhile, we can make *some* progress without Helsing," said Rupert. "Your hand is next to my right pocket, Orlov. Can you reach inside it?"

"I've already got a pocket of my own," said Orlov, stupidly.

"Orlov!" hissed Rupert. "It's not the pocket itself that interests me. It's the penknife inside."

"Ooh, that sounds useful," grinned Orlov. "We could cut the ropes with it."

"That *is* the general idea, Orlov!"

Retrieving the penknife from Rupert's pocket was very easy for the multi-fingered Orlov.

"Done!" said Orlov. "What now?"

"Free yourself, then us," said Rupert.

Within minutes, all of them were off the slab and rubbing sore wrists and ankles.

"FREEDOM!" cried Orlov.

"Hush!" said Klaw. "Someone's coming."

They now all could hear the tip-tapping of footsteps from the room behind the wall.

"Grog!" hissed Rupert. "I'd recognize that sound anywhere. Quick. Back on the slab."

"But we've just got free," protested Orlov. Rupert pulled him roughly back on the slab.

Grog was not alone. Soon after entering the room, Krinkelfiend silently appeared. And, more silently still, Vlad Dracula.

"My lord," said Krinkelfiend, "here are the

prisoners, minus Helsing, as promised."

Dracula stepped forwards towards the slab; so tall, so dignified, so graceful, he seemed to float. "Good evening, inquisitive visitors," said Dracula. "You are very privileged to be witnessing this unique moment." Dracula examined the slab upon which they lay. "And Helsing hasn't returned yet?" he asked. No one answered. "A pity, for he will miss the fun. And if he thinks he can do something to interfere. . . Well, once my powers are complete, not even an Immortal One can stand in the way of Vlad Basarab III. However." He turned to Grog. "Grog. Check the vicinity. Make sure Helsing isn't planning some heroic but pointless intrusion."

Without answering, Grog clicked his way from the cellar to search the palace.

Dracula turned to Krinkelfiend, who was carrying a large varnished wooden case in both arms. "The case, Krinkelfiend."

"Yes, Master."

Krinkelfiend brought the case forward as Dracula clicked his fingers. At once a table appeared in the room, and the case was placed upon it. "Open!" he instructed the case, which immediately obeyed his command.

Everyone turned their heads to try to peer at the glimmering contents.

"Oh, yes," gushed Krinkelfiend. "The two daggers!"

"I had expected there to be three," said the professor from the slab.

"All in good time, Herr von Morcumstein," said Dracula, without taking his gaze from the magnificent daggers.

A shuffling sound came from the other section of the room. "And now, Herr Professor," said Dracula, "you might be interested in meeting Marvin, the blind monk."

The professor, beside himself with excitement, craned his head backwards to glimpse the monk, who had now entered the dimly lit room.

Marvin was covered by his monk's habit, so it was difficult to see *any*thing of him behind the floppy brown robe and large hood. He stopped between Krinkelfiend and Dracula in front of the table.

"A remarkable man, was ... *is* –" Dracula corrected himself – "Marvin. Born blind, but with unique power. The power to suck energy from the atmosphere by meditation, and transfer it to any object of his – or rather, *my* – choice. Hence," said Dracula, peering down at the open case, "my perfect daggers."

"I've often wondered how Marvin executed his control over energy," said the professor, as if they were having a discussion over the dinner table after a pleasant meal. "I presume his mind goes into a trance, during which he commands the atmosphere to obey him."

"Quite so," said Dracula. "And he transfers this mass of force into the ruby jewel of each dagger."

Marvin then produced the third dagger from his habit. The professor noted the dagger was identical to the other two, but most of his attention, and that of his colleagues, was focused on the silent, hooded Marvin. The professor was fascinated to be in the presence of the famous monk who had lived so long ago, and he couldn't help but marvel at Dracula's remarkable skills at bringing him back to life.

The third dagger was laid on the table next to the other two. "And now the power of these daggers will combine and transfer their energy into me. For centuries I have waited patiently for this moment. The moment when my *own* powers were great enough to summon Marvin from his resting place and continue our venture into darkness. My revenge on mortal man is now about to be completed. *I* alone will become the holder of phenomenal energies. One hundred years of darkness will follow. The world will turn to night. So it was written all those years ago, is that not so, Marvin?" Marvin said and did nothing. He appeared to be no more than a walking zombie, merely returned to walk the earth and complete the work he had begun all those centuries ago.

"Get ready to throw yourself on the floor," whispered the professor to Rupert. "Tell the others."

Dracula laid one blade against the other till all three were in union. "The parchment," he said to Krinkelfiend, who quickly produced an old piece of paper from his pocket. Dracula took it, and read the ancient vampire psalm that was written down.

He muttered the words beneath his breath, his eyes flickering wildly. And, as he spoke, the

Burmese ruby in the hilt of each dagger began to glow brighter and brighter, illuminating Dracula's pale features.

Sparks began leaping out from the rubies with little fizzing sounds. "Get ready!" said the professor to Helsing. Then the sparks turned to flames, and Dracula twitched as three shafts of light combined as one shimmering golden ray, and thrust themselves through Dracula's chest and out through his back like a massive sword.

"NOW!" called the professor, and the prisoners tossed themselves to the floor, rolling beneath the slab for cover.

Krinkelfiend took a step towards the prisoners, but faltered, torn between stopping them and watching helplessly as his master seemed to burn up before his eyes.

Then the daggers started to spin upon the table, faster and faster, until, with a mighty, deafening explosion, one of them blew apart into tiny fragments, a thousand lethal weapons whizzing around the cellar.

"KEEP YOUR HEAD DOWN!" warned Rupert.

Dracula seemed to grow in stature, as the energy flew around the room in a long blue vibrating finger, finally entering his forehead. "YES! YES!" he cried. "POWER!"

Suddenly Marvin the blind monk grabbed one of the two remaining weapons and thrust it deep into Dracula's chest. "AAARGH!" cried the king of all vampires, falling to his knees. Then Marvin withdrew the dagger and threw it and its counterpart away. He sprinted over to the crouched figures beneath the slab to take cover.

"Er, Marvin?" stammered the professor.

"Helsing, actually," smiled Helsing, tossing back his hood. "Marvin and I caught up on old times, and he agreed to help me out. It's taken four hundred years to have a second chance, but—"

Helsing was interrupted by the mighty explosions of the two remaining daggers. Dracula was now in flames, toxic smoke pouring from his fiery body, the air turning thick and making them all choke.

Grog dashed back into the room. "DUCK!" called Krinkelfiend, and he and Grog did precisely that.

A piece of dagger shrapnel flew past the

professor's ear and straight into Helsing's stomach.
"Ouch!" said Helsing. "That hurt!"

"Hurt!" cried Orlov. "If you were a normal person, it would have killed you!"

Dracula let out a mad scream, which jolted everyone in the room. And then the four-hundred-year-old lord of all vampires exploded with a deafening crack, which shook the walls of the cellar.

In the choking smoke and chaos following, there was nothing left to find of what had been Vlad Dracula. Not even a scrap of cape or a piece of top hat. The combined powers of the three mighty daggers, plus a bit of interference from Helsing, the Immortal One, had sealed Dracula's fate. He had been totally atomized where he had stood.

He raised his lethal fingers at his son, and flung all his mighty powers towards him.

✧ Chapter Fourteen
Journey's End

King Konstantine stroked his long, long beard, which reached down to his toes. "What a mess!" he commented, on observing piles of dust around his feet. "How did *that* get in here?"

His daughter, Princess Lashka, rushed into the king's room. "Papa, you are all right?"

"Never felt better," said the king. "Why?"

"We were turned to stone."

"Were we? How strange!"

"It is true, Your Majesty," said Walter, appearing at the king's door. "The one who did this to us is the same person who visited the palace some years ago."

"Oh, *him*," grumbled the king. "The chap who helped himself to my favourite port. Cheeky devil. I'll have a thing or two to tell *him* when I catch him."

Back in the cellar, the smoke was clearing. "Up the ladder!" called Helsing to his friends.

Krinkelfiend and Grog lunged at the escaping men, but missed, and instead collided with each other in an untidy heap of legs, wooden legs, and arms.

Orlov was last through the hatch into the palace corridor. Orlov, who was now handsome and strong.

"You did it!" said Orlov, patting Rupert heartily on the back, almost hurting him.

"I did?" said Rupert. Then he looked more closely at Orlov. "You. . . You're beautiful again, Orlov. A piece of a dagger must have struck you."

Orlov held up a jagged piece of metal and smiled, a big, toothy, handsome smile. "In my left leg," he smiled. "I could tell at once I was changing. All that realized energy firing through my body."

"YOU CAUSED THIS!" Krinkelfiend cried furiously at Rupert, as he emerged, dusty and battered, from the top of the hatch. "You killed my poor master. You. . . You. . ." He didn't know quite what to say, he was so angry.

"Father, I suggest we all calm down and behave sensibly," said Rupert. Grog climbed up to the floor and clicked nimbly towards Rupert, his hands outstretched, his face red and furious. But he didn't reach Rupert. Orlov picked him up as if he were no more than a bag of feathers, and hung him on a hook on the wall. "You can stay there till you calm down!" Orlov told him. Grog was too surprised to say anything.

But Krinkelfiend was quicker and wiser. He cast a spell that knocked everyone to the ground – except his son, with whom he wanted to deal personally.

Krinkelfiend then flung himself at his son's throat in a flash of black top hat and cape.

"Calm down, Father. . ." Rupert began, which was followed by, "Garragh!" as his father's fingers tightened around his neck.

167

"You and your meddling friends," cried Krinkelfiend, beside himself with anger and frustration. "Garragh!" repeated Rupert, his head shaking limply to and fro. "What have you done? What have you done?" bellowed Krinkelfiend. "Dracula is no more!"

Then there was a puff of purple smoke, and Krinkelfiend discovered he was now throttling thin air.

Rupert flew off down the corridor, as quickly as his wings would take him.

"*Two* can play at *that* game!" snarled Krinkelfiend. And he, too, burst into bat-form and flew off after his fleeing son.

Rupert didn't know quite what he should do. The thought crossed his mind that this wasn't the first time that they had chased each other around the palace disguised as bats. But there wasn't time to ponder the irony of this. It was his survival that concerned him. There was no telling what nightmarish spell his father would put on him if he was caught. And Rupert knew that his father's powers had always been greater than his own.

"Come back here!" growled Krinkelfiend, flying

into room after room, knocking over chairs and tables as he relentlessly chased poor Rupert.

Then Krinkelfiend flew into the ballroom, transforming into human shape. The room was big and silent, but he was certain he had seen his son fly in there just before him. "I know you're here!" said Krinkelfiend, sounding more certain than he actually was. "You can't hide from me for long."

Krinkelfiend heard a gentle rustling behind him, and immediately spun around, blasting a "destruct" spell in that direction. The French windows blew off their hinges, leaving the curtains sizzling and smoking in their wake. But the rustling had been no more than the curtains themselves, caught in a tiny draught.

"What the deuce is going on in my ballroom?" demanded the king, entering the room, hands on hips. "I bet you're the rotten egg who once helped himself to my port, eh?"

Krinkelfiend, hardly bothering to look in King Konstantine's direction, clicked his fingers and sent him running from the room with his long beard on fire.

Suddenly his eyes landed upon a portrait hanging above a large fireplace. There was something very familiar about the painting. Suddenly, the figure in the portrait raised an arm and fired a spell at Krinkelfiend, which knocked the vampire off his feet and sent him spinning across the slippery ballroom floor. Rupert then jumped out of the portrait, which he had cloaked, and darted, in human form, for the corridor. But not before his father unleashed a shot from his fingers as he lay crumpled on the ballroom floor.

The streak of red force hit Rupert on an ankle, upending him, and he fell with a heavy crash that left him winded and sore.

"Aha!" grinned Krinkelfiend, scrambling to his feet and skipping over to his son. "Now I have the meddling fool where I want him."

"Father, please behave yourself," puffed Rupert, exhausted and frightened. "The daggers are destroyed. It's all over."

But his words just made Krinkelfiend angrier still. He raised his lethal fingers at his son, and flung all his mighty powers towards him. But all his mighty powers amounted to very little.

"Eh?" muttered Krinkelfiend, looking quizzically at his useless fingers.

"The daggers!" laughed Rupert, climbing delicately to his feet.

"What of them?" demanded Krinkelfiend.

"When they combined their powers, they must have begun to drain both of *ours*."

"WHAT!" screamed Krinkelfiend, aghast at the thought.

"He's quite right," said Professor von Morcumstein, who, along with Helsing, Orlov and Inspector Klaw, had joined the fighting vampires in the corridor. "*All* our energies have been drained, I imagine," he went on, as if he were lecturing students. "The daggers survived on the energy that Marvin collected through his mystical powers, and any passing energy surrounding them. That was why Dracula kept his contact with the daggers to a minimum, keeping the first one locked away in a cubbyhole. And it would explain why you were once absorbed by the first dagger in the Tryfoolian mountain range. And there you might have remained, had not a poor shepherd chanced to free you. And then," continued the professor with a little cough, "there came the coming together of the *three*. What folly! It was just too much. When they exploded, their trapped energies returned to the atmosphere, taking with it, it appears, all of ours, too!"

"But you're not a vampire," said Krinkelfiend, angrily.

"Precisely," said the professor. "So for us the difference is non-existent. It is *you* who will find things very different from now on."

"Why did you have to spoil everything?" sobbed Krinkelfiend, falling to his knees and burying his face in his hands. "My life was perfect till *you* lot interfered again."

"Now, now, Father," said Rupert, patting his parent on the back. "Let's put on a brave face, eh? Having no powers might be just the thing to put you on the road to being a better person. And anyway, it's not exactly the end of the world, is it?"

"Exactly!" cried Krinkelfiend through a huge sob.

Helsing, Klaw, Rupert and Orlov stood on the platform of Grund station and said their goodbyes to Professor von Morcumstein. Orlov, poor Orlov. The magic had worn off as quickly as the energy from the exploded daggers had dispersed.

"Strong, handsome, clever, wonderful . . . for five minutes," moaned Orlov. "Just *five* minutes!"

"I'm sorry," said Rupert, patting the hump on Orlov's deformed shoulder. "If it is any consolation, Orlov," he smiled, "you will always be beautiful to me. Beauty comes from within."

"Really?" sighed Orlov, and he smiled the kind of smile that would crack a thousand mirrors.

"I suppose we'll never meet again," said Klaw, reaching in through the carriage window and shaking the professor by the hand.

"Never say never," smiled the professor. "And who knows. Should Krinkelfiend miraculously recover his vampire powers, *any*thing might happen."

"ALL ABOARD WHO IS GOING ABOARD!" shouted the station master.

"I thought you might like to know that the king and his daughter, Princess Lashka, send you their thanks and best wishes, Professor," said Helsing.

"Most kind, I'm sure," nodded the professor.

"I do hope the king's beard grows back!"

"The palace returned to normal, *and* no more Dracula," said Klaw. "It's almost too good to believe. My chief will be the happiest man in the land."

"The funny thing about it," said the professor, "is that Dracula could have had all the power he had wanted, should he have stayed with the two daggers. He just got greedy, and it cost him his life."

"That is what the poor brilliant Marvin explained to me," said Helsing. "Marvin was furious and desperate that he should not be allowed to rest even though his mortal life had long ended. So he had the idea to destroy Dracula once and for all. All he had to do was go along with the plan to make a third dagger. Marvin knew the combined power would be too great."

"And I imagine Marvin was pleased to reacquaint himself with you," said the professor.

"He was somewhat surprised, especially when I told him how many years had passed since our last meeting."

"What became of Marvin after you disguised yourself as him?" asked Klaw.

"Vaporized!" said Helsing. "You must understand, he was never really alive again, you know. Dracula merely brought his image back from the grave. As soon as Dracula vaporized, anything he had full control of did likewise."

"How sad," said Klaw.

"Not really," smiled Helsing. "I'm sure *none* of us want to be disturbed from our long and permanent sleep."

"That is something you will possibly never know," chuckled the professor, and Helsing just laughed.

The guard blew his whistle, and the sixteen-coach train hooted, and in a puff of suffocating smoke, eased along its rails.

"GOODBYE!" called the figures on the platform.

"*Au revoir!*" replied the professor, and sat down to enjoy his long journey back home – back to the small town of Muhlhausen.

Epilogue

Helsing settled back in Bran, and is currently looking into other vampire cases he has heard talk of. Professor von Morcumstein has retired from active adventure, and occasionally gives speeches about his life to enthusiastic audiences in the Muhlhausen town hall. He is also amending his work on vampire lore. Inspector Klaw was promoted to Chief Inspector Klaw – the youngest in the history of the Gertcha police force. Rupert proposed to Princess Lashka, and they were married despite his lack of aristocratic roots. They are now living at Viktoria Palace with King Konstantine. Orlov is employed there, as he is as fond of Rupert as Rupert is of him. And Orlov wishes that maybe one day he will be beautiful again. Strangely, with each passing day, he cares less about that wish coming true. He knows that, whatever he looks like, he is happy and he is loved.

Count Arnold Krinkelfiend, still lacking his amazing vampire skills, is being held in a secure prison on the edge of Gertcha. He looks older than ever before, and appears to be a broken man. But inside his head he is planning . . . planning . . . planning. . .